Book One of The Deception Series

Web

Of

I0676841

Deception

Ryan Hodge

SMP
PUBLISHING

SMP Publishing Edition

Printed in the United States of America

10 9 8 7 6 5 4 3 2 1

ISBN: 978-0692428399 (PBK)

DEDICATION

Dear Ma,

You always taught me that I could be anything, see everywhere, and do anything. In a life filled with struggles, you inspired me to transcend the struggle and beat the odds. Your optimistic words and willingness to face adversity head on is why I am who I am today. You and your unwavering message guide me even in your going home.

"If it ain't rough, it ain't right,"
Is what mom would tell us when things got tight.
That line informed us that things won't always go
your way,
But you still gotta fight and make it to the next day.
She would repeat "If you gonna do it, do it right,"
She was small in stature, but had a lion's might.
Always optimistic in all that she did,
When adversity hit, she never ran, never hid.
We are now guided by your teachings and watched by
your spirit,
We wish you were still with us, so your voice we
could hear it.
We miss the days of giving you a ring,
And when you answer the phone, hearing you say,
"Everything, Everything."
We throw up our love,
Cause we know you are looking down from the
heavens up above.

CHAPTER 1

An attractive woman should not be without sex or a man. It just isn't right. It's been such a long time since I last had sex, that I really don't remember much about it. It was sometime in the past year I guess, but it seems like it was years ago. My body is telling me that I'm well overdue for some serious attention. My sweet spot has been throbbing and twitching like crazy and sex is all I can think of. I often find myself caressing my body as I visualize how he feels, smells, and tastes. My vagina is flowing like a faucet just thinking about it. I need to feel a man inside of me now. I don't need to feel him for very long. I don't need an hour or even thirty minutes for that matter, although that would be nice. I really just need about five minutes to feel a strong man with gentle hands all over my body. I want him to passionately explore every inch of my body and slowly push his veined filled penis inside of me. I want to feel my body explode like the Hoover Dam being destroyed by dynamite. Is that too much to ask? The way my hormones are raging I know I will burst in two minutes tops. Hell, as long as it's been, I may even have two eruptions in five minutes.

I feel so guilty thinking like this. Growing up in a Christian household, this would never be acceptable. My grandmother would roll over in her grave ten times if she knew the thoughts I'm having. I need to get this off of my mind. Maybe I should go to the gym. To the gym - where there are sexy, toned, and sweaty men all around. Well, obviously that's not the answer. My body is tingling all over thinking about it, but I absolutely refuse to use another sex toy. To be honest, they really aren't hitting the spot anymore. I've tried them all and none are a good substitute for the real thing. Getting an orgasm from my dildo is taking longer and longer and my "bullet" just isn't firing the way it used to. I need a man to stroke me deeply. I need him to slightly choke me, run his fingers through my hair, and gently nibble on my body. I want him to bend me over and thrust me repeatedly, all while he grabs and smacks my ass. Where is the man who will do it the way it needs to be done?

As I lay in bed, my mind is racing and I just can't get comfortable. My bed used to be very relaxing and sleeping wasn't a problem. I spent a lot of money to purchase a top of the line memory foam mattress which is designed to contour to the curvature of my body. The truth is there's nothing physically wrong with my bed. It's just that my bed is cold and lonely and I'm tired of talking to and cuddling with my stuffed animals. Unfortunately, teddy bears don't squeeze back. I have the need to feel a warm body next to mine. I'm anxiously waiting to feel a man's heartbeat up against my chest and sweat dripping from our bodies after a mind blowing sexual encounter. I covet the feeling of him lifting up my "hood" and massaging my special prize until I burst on his tongue. Bottom line, I need body to body and groin to groin comingling action.

I definitely believe this is a two-way street and I'm all about pleasing my man. I will ride his dick and tighten my vagina around it until he releases a manly scream and discharges his swim team into my swimming pool. But as much as I want to release all of this energy I have built up inside of me, it can't be with just any random man. I refuse to give my body to another man too soon. Although it's happened before, I have to stay strong and not allow my sexual urges to take over my better judgment. The next man to get my loving will have to earn it! No ifs, ands, or buts about it. He will be getting too much from me to not have to work for it. He has to be on point in all aspects. He will have to be a good person, a man of God, and out of this world handsome. Additionally, he can't be a player. I am tired of these men who think women are only here to serve as their personal amusement park. Those days are over.

I definitely need some badly though and finding the right guy will not be an overnight endeavor. This could be a long and time consuming process. I have to mentally prepare myself as I'm sure I'll be let down before I find the guy I'm looking for, but that's life. I'll be damned if I pick up anymore numbers to my sexual partners' list just to get a temporary fix. I already added two more to the list that I didn't plan to. Those relationships didn't last longer than six months a piece. I listened to my body and I gave them the goods even though my mind told me not to. Of course, shortly thereafter the relationship was over.

I could give my ex-boyfriend a call. He's *always* available when I need him. I know for sure he will take care of my body the way I need him to. I can certainly say he never disappoints in that arena. Unfortunately, he doesn't deserve to have me in a sexual fashion because our relationship will never be more than just that - sex. We have very little in common and I always feel guilty about having sex with him knowing we have no future together. He's not ready for a serious relationship and I'm at a point in my life where that's important. However, calling him will have my needs met and keep me from adding another partner to my list. I need to stop relying on him for a sexual fix when I'm in between guys. It's so difficult because he's always been a good standby. Whenever I call, he's more than willing to oblige my request with no hard feelings and no questions asked.

Oh my goodness, what should I do? I am *not* calling my ex. I need to get serious about finding a man, a real man, a life partner, a husband. I need someone who wants the same things in life that I want. I need someone who wants to build a future with me and have a family. I have to get empowered and take charge of my situation. I can no longer afford to be weak and give in to these sexual urges I have.

What I need to do is put myself in position to meet new and exciting people. I need to get more engaged in community events and stop being so antisocial. I really need to get back on my workout schedule too. I'm normally very upbeat and energetic when I'm a few pounds thinner. If I'm going on the hunt, I need to be in top form. The better I look and feel will increase my chances of successfully meeting someone who looks good too. They say you attract what you exude. Not sure who "they" are, but the saying works for me. Sitting in the house being lazy and making excuses will not help me attain my desired goal.

I have to switch my mentality from thinking

someone will find me or God will send someone to me. Those thoughts haven't worked for me so far. It's almost like thinking I'm going to win the lottery without purchasing a ticket. I have to play the game to put myself in a position to win. I won't find a man by being passive. Don't get me wrong, I'm not saying I'll be overly aggressive in my search, but I will surely be assertive and confident. Most importantly, I can't come off as eager or desperate. That could be a turn off and some men may pick up on it and try to use it against me.

So let me think. Where can I go to meet nice guys? I need to figure out some places around town to frequent. In the Mix is always jumping and filled with guys who are successful, but that's where Sage works and that obviously didn't work out for me. I don't really want to go back there because of the memories it brings back, but it's a very nice place and something to keep on the radar. I wonder if the club scene is the best place for me to meet a man who's worthy of me. I don't necessarily think I'm better than anyone, but I do have a lot to offer and I should have high standards. A woman has to have standards, otherwise anything is acceptable.

A lot of people say, "Don't pick up guys at the club because nobody worth anything is at the club." I disagree because I'm a good person who loves the club scene. That's not to say that I go to clubs to seek out men, but that's definitely a place where men hang out. Let's be clear, not all men who go to the club are dogs or are even on the hunt to find women. Some men go to clubs just to hang out with their friends, much like women do - much like I do. I need to put that misconception out of my mind and not limit my options. Where else can I go other than the club? There are plenty of cocktail hours at upscale restaurants around town and I hear there are poetry nights at the local university all the time. There has to be a bunch of upstanding guys there. I'm sure when I renew my gym membership there will be potential candidates in there too. Yes, definitely. Sexy men who care about their bodies and will hopefully revere mine. I just need a little exposure and my personality, intellect, and banging body will do the rest.

I guess I'll also have to be open to the possibility of dating older or younger guys. I am 27 years old and I want a long term relationship, so I need to keep all of my options open. Why cut off an entire selection pool because of age? It's settled. I am going to be a social butterfly. The days of riding in the passenger seat are over for me. It's time to put on the driving gloves and hit the road. Look out D.C., Sheena Mills is on the scene and looking for love!

I know I can't attend all of these venues by myself. It's just too dangerous for an attractive female to be out alone at night. I may look vulnerable and people are crazy! I don't want to be an easy target and have men preying on me. I'm going to have to lean on my girls heavy for this. I'm glad they aren't in my situation of being single, but it makes it a little more challenging for us to hang out. I don't want to cause friction in their relationships, but they have to help me with this position I'm in. It may be somewhat difficult for them to understand why I'm doing this, but I need them now more than ever. First, I'll draft a tentative schedule for us to hang out. This will be a guide to help us make appearances at the spots when they're most popping. I hope my girls come through for me. "No" isn't an option in this case. I'll make the schedule to include different times, so I'll get more exposure while not tying them up too much.

Let me give the girls a call to let them know what I'm thinking and to see if they can get free to help with my quest. I'm calling Ilesha first since I'm right by her house. I think this is something I should discuss with them in person.

"Hey girl. What you up to?" I ask.

Ilesha replies, "Hey, I'm home on the sofa. It's too hot outside and I just got my hair done. I am not trying to sweat out my curls."

"Girl, I hear you. I have the AC on full blast. Listen, I need to stop by and talk to you about something," I reply.

"Here we go! What's wrong? Come over now!" Ilesha demands.

I say, "Calm down girl. It's nothing bad. It

could actually be a good thing. I'll be there in like ten minutes."

"Oh okay, but it sounds urgent. I'm gonna call Rachel and tell her to come over too. I just bought some more liquor, so we can have a few drinks while we chat," Ilesha narrates.

This is working out better than I planned. I didn't want to inconvenience my girls and have a formal meeting, but it's coming together without me having to do much at all. My girls are wonderful. They always tell me what is right for me as opposed to telling me what I want to hear. They both accomplish the same thing, but go about it differently. For example, Ilesha is more straight-forward with her advice giving. She tells you exactly what's on her mind with no sugarcoating. You have to be ready for the raw and uncut conversations with her. Ilesha is a real firecracker and is very aggressive. To the contrary, Rachel is more laid back and reserved. She gets what she wants in a more meticulous manner. For example, she will tell you when you are making a bad decision, but she won't tell you harshly. Her word choice is very tactful and well chosen. If she wants to tell a person that he or she is making a poor decision, she often tells a story about someone who has been in a similar situation first. She then uses that story to transition into how it relates to you. When it's all said and done, both of my girls tell me what I need to hear, even if it's not what I want to hear.

Ilesha, Rachel, and I have been the tightest of friends for a very long time. I'm so blessed to have them in my life. I met them both when I moved to a section of town called Up Linden in the seventh grade. Fortunately for me, we ended up in the same science class. At first I didn't really say much, since I didn't know anyone at the school. Rachel and Ilesha sat next to each other and seemed to be pretty good friends. I couldn't understand why they were so close because they seemed so different from one another. Just a couple of days into the school year, Ilesha and Rachel entered the classroom and Ilesha complimented me on my outfit and my style in general. In class I always thought Ilesha was a little loud and ghetto, and even though she could dress too, I never would have approached her first. But after that, we really got to know each other and began hanging out together outside of school. It began to make sense why Rachel and Ilesha were such good friends. They both were a lot of fun and balanced each other out. I was just that additional oomph their duo needed. We did everything together and remained the best of friends all the way through our schooling. We even decided to go to college together. Our relationships were so strong that we roomed together during our first three years of college. Many people advised us not to do it if we wanted to remain friends, but we did anyway. We had each other's backs back then and the same still exists today.

We don't always see eye to eye on everything, but they are sisters to me. They know all of my most intimate secrets and I theirs. They were around for my first real kiss, my first boyfriend, and my first experience with a man. Our relationship reminds me of a marriage. We support each other through good times, bad times and in sickness and in health. They are the type of women to split their last with you because they don't want you to have to go without. I remember when we were in college during our freshman year and I had a situation where somehow my meal plan was canceled and I didn't have any money or food to eat. Ilesha and Rachel came to the rescue. They shared their food with me every day until I was able to get my dilemma rectified. Sometimes we only had ramen noodles and pop tarts to eat, but we shared those too. Times in college were hard, but we had each other so things were never too bad.

I recall during our college years how we would always swap clothes. To be truthful, every now and then we still do. We would even let the other one keep an outfit if we felt like she looked better in it. In other instances, we would preclude each other from wearing certain outfits because it wasn't a good fit or it just looked ridiculous. We had a pact to never let each other look like fools. Nobody violated the pact and things were pleasant among us for the most part.

I pull up to Ilesha's house and toot the horn, so she knows I'm here. I see Rachel's car parked along the street. Rachel drives a small compact car which is so symmetrical with her personality. She is not flashy or flamboyant. Since I've known her, she has only worn makeup three times. She has a natural beauty though, and doesn't like or need any extra adornments. I park in the driveway next to Ilesha's car. Her car is a perfect reflection of her personality too. Ilesha drives a red Escalade with rims on it. Her presence is always felt and so is the car she drives. It is loud and bold just like she is. She even has a speaker system in it that is very thunderous. You can hear her and her car coming from blocks away. I get out the car and walk into the house.

When I walk inside, Ilesha and Rachel are sitting at the kitchen table drinking cocktails already.

I say, "Well damn! You couldn't wait for me? Bunch of damn alcoholics! Early as hell and already drinking."

"I'm sorry girl. I wanted to wait, but this drink was calling me. You know how I feel about my amaretto sours! And it has cherries in it," Rachel explains.

Ilesha, staying true to form states, "Bitch please. You were taking too long to get here. Plus, there is plenty to go around. Ain't no sorry. Better get you a drink."

We all erupt into laughter. I can always count

on Ilesha to keep it real and certainly keep us entertained. I walk over to the counter to carefully construct my amaretto sour. It has to have the perfect combination of the liqueur and sweet & sour mix and naturally I put a lot of cherries in it. The cherries are the best part. I love the way they taste after they absorb the liqueur. Ilesha, knowing her girls, began soaking them as soon as I called her.

Ilesha says, "Okay girl. You got your drink fixed. What's going on? When you called, you said you had something on your mind. Spill the damn beans!"

Rachel says, "Ilesha, don't pressure her. She will tell us when she feels comfortable. It's alright Sheena, take your time."

I say, "It's really not that serious. Nothing is really going on. I just need your help with something."

"Girl, you know we are here for you. What do you need help with?" Rachel asks.

I respond, "Well, you know I have been single for quite some time and I've decided that it's time for me to start dating again." I look down, take a sip of my drink and sigh, "I need a man."

"Yeah, you need a man, but more importantly, you need some dick!" says Ilesha.

Rachel curtly replies, "She didn't say that!" As she realizes her tone, she calmly continues, "She just wants to be in a committed relationship. That's all."

I quickly reply, "I do want a relationship badly, but a nice long hard dick would be what the doctor ordered too."

Ilesha starts laughing and giving me support for wanting sex. Rachel blushes and begins to chuckle as well. The drinks are starting to take a toll on us. I don't drink much, so my tolerance is extremely low. Rachel has a higher tolerance than me, but she's already had more drinks than I have. Since Ilesha overdoes everything, she has had more drinks than Rachel and I combined.

"See, I told you she wants to get her back blown out! But Sheena, you didn't say what you need us to help you with," says Ilesha.

"I need you two to help me meet some good men," I say.

"Oh, you want us to hook you up with somebody?" asks Rachel. "I know plenty of guys from work," she continues.

I explain to them that I do not wish to be hooked up with anyone and I just want them to be available to hang out. I also tell them about a girls' night out schedule that I'm working on.

"Sheena, a schedule? Really?" Ilesha asks.

Rachel says, "That is a bit unconventional, but I'm okay with it."

I reply, "Yes, a schedule. Listen to me. If we have a schedule, it becomes much easier to stick to. You can plan around it and you will be able to let me know which nights work for you. Then we can proceed accordingly. You will also be able to let your boyfriends know in advance that we're hanging out. I really need your help. It's not like I can just roam the streets alone."

"Girl, is that it? You just need us to hang with you? You know I like to be out anyway. My dude will just have to understand. Besides, all I gotta do is suck his dick real good and his ass will be happy as hell and then fast asleep," says Ilesha.

"Ilesha, you are so nasty! Keep that mess in your bedroom!" Rachel says.

Ilesha grinds her lower body and replies, "I keep it in the bedroom, the bathroom, the kitchen, and anywhere else I can get it!"

We all fall out laughing again. I love my girls; they are irreplaceable!

Rachel says, "Girl, your request is small. I thought you were going to ask for something big."

Ilesha chimes in, "Yeah, as dramatic as you were, I thought you were going to ask for ten thousand dollars or something."

Rachel continues, "Girl, you know I got your back. I'll talk to my man later just to inform him that I will be hanging out a little more than normal. No big deal."

I thank them and we continue our mid-day drinks. I'm really glad they are so supportive. I'm also excited because girl time is something that we don't get a lot of these days. We are really tight like sisters, but since college we've moved into our separate lives. It amazes me how we all live in Washington, D.C., but don't get to see each other that often. It's easy for us to get busy with what we have going on and sometimes it's almost like we live in different states. With that being said, we always come through for one another when we're needed.

I am a business owner, which is very arduous and time consuming. I love my job, but I have many employees who need managing and tutelage. I pride myself in developing young talent. I also teach a business class at the local university. My time is spread thin, but one thing I know is that people find time for who or what they feel is important. Therefore, I will find the time to meet someone special. Rachel's job is also demanding. She is the chief human resources officer for her company. She's always in meetings and in airports. Since her company is located in many major US cities, she's always on the go. She's constantly traveling to meet new clients, evaluate the local HR offices, or sometimes fire current employees. Her responsibilities seem endless, but she loves what she does and she's great at it. Ilesha's career is perfect for her too. She's a nationally syndicated radio show host. She spends her days telling people exactly what's on her mind, whether solicited or not. She also hosts many events all over the country and is an absolute professional when it comes to her career. None of us have any children. We are still trying to build our careers, so having kids right now just isn't part of the plan. For now, our careers are our kids.

D.C. is an ideal place to be. One of the things I love about D.C. is that there's always something to do. There's a tremendous amount of history here and it has the best museums. The nightlife can also rival any US city's nightlife. Additionally, since it is the nation's capital, there's a constant influx of new people. One way to look at it is that the constant influx will increase my chances of meeting new people. Handsome, professional, and goal oriented men are continuously in the city. All I have to do is find one.

After we finish our drinks, we hug and demand that we text each other once Rachel and I make it home safely. That's something we always do when we go out and it definitely applies today since we've been drinking. I leave Ilesha's house and drive back home. I didn't go overboard on the drinks at her house because I knew I had to drive. As I pull into my garage, I quickly send a text to the girls to let them know I'm home. Just a few minutes later I receive a similar text from Rachel and a message from Ilesha that states, "Bout damn time! Later chicks!" When I get into the house, I grab my tablet and curl up on the couch. I'm looking for venues that cater to the professional crowd. I want a companion, but I don't want just anyone. We have to be evenly yoked. I'm compiling a list of possible places we can go. There are different things going on all over the city at different times, so we'll have a busy schedule ahead of us. I'm conference calling them now to give them a preview of our girls' night out schedule.

"Hey, I put together a schedule of places for us to go. There are a bunch of different upcoming events for us to attend. We can hit up the homecoming, poetry night, and the all-white party, just to name of few," I report.

Ilesha says, "I haven't been to an all-white party in forever. They were the shit back in the day. I'm ready to go now!"

Rachel chimes in, "We did have a good time at those. Everyone would be eloquently dressed and on their best behavior. There wasn't any nonsense at those parties. The music was always suitable for dancing and we would dance all night."

I say, "Yeah, none of that ratchet and ghetto music. I hope those parties haven't changed much since a few years ago."

"I would leave those parties drenched in sweat. Couldn't keep me off the dance floor. I know I had to have lost five pounds from partying there," says Ilesha.

"Five pounds! Yeah, you may have lost five pounds, but it wasn't from dancing. It was from giving it up to all of those dudes afterwards," I retort.

Rachel says, "Ooh, you're wrong for that."

Ilesha states, "It is what it is. I was young and

living in the moment. I had a lot of fun and good times. I wouldn't change any of the things I did back then. If I didn't experience those times back then, I wouldn't be the diva I am today. Besides, why wouldn't I share my pure pleasure with a few good men?"

"I hear you girl. Do what you do! You know we don't judge you and never have. We all have our desires," Rachel says.

I reply, "Ain't that the truth?"

I've always been a very sexual person, but I've tried to suppress my desires for fear of being labeled a whore or a thot. Ilesha has never had that problem. She never cared about what others thought of her and still doesn't. Since I can remember, I've been the "good girl" which comes with a lot of pressure and expectations.

"Listen I gotta do some running, so I'm getting off the phone. But check your emails. I sent both of you a calendar of what's going on. That's our itinerary," I say.

"Okay. I'll check it when we hang up," says Rachel.

"I'll check it after I finish with my babe. He's ringing the doorbell now. I'm bout to get me some!" says Ilesha in a singing tone.

We all say bye and end the call.

CHAPTER 2

The first place on our list of places to scout is an all-white party. An all-white party is a party with a very specific dress code. In order to gain entry to the party, you have to be dressed in all white garments. The only part of your outfit that doesn't have to be white is your accessories. I'm excited about the party because we haven't been to one of these parties in years. We always had fun because the music was slamming and people's minds were in the right spirit. Knuckleheads were never at these parties seemingly because it required guests to dress up. Additionally, I'm stoked about the party because of the caliber of men who used to be there. If things remain the same as the past, there will be many viable candidates for me at the party. The party will be at the Upscale Hotel this year. This is one of the most beautiful hotels in our nation's capital. The banquet hall where the party is being held can hold several hundred people.

The tickets to the event are pricey, but I purchase them anyway. I feel it's for a good cause; the good cause is I need a man. I'm not getting any younger and my eggs certainly have a shelf life. I have to use them while they're still good. I hope my future boyfriend or husband is at this party. Hell, I'll be happy to at least get some good conversation going.

The party is tonight and I need to find something to wear. I check my closet to see what's in it. I could wear this outfit, but I don't know if I want to wear pants or not. This dress looks good, but I'll have to wear my hair up for it to look right and I really want to wear my hair down. I have nothing in here to wear. I know Rachel already knows what she's wearing. She's had her outfit picked out for at least a week because she's not a procrastinator when it comes to anything. Let me call Ilesha and see what she's wearing.

"Hey, what you doing?" I ask.

"Nothing, sitting here trying to figure out what I'm wearing tonight. What you up to?" Ilesha asks.

"Same thing. Looking for something to wear, but ain't nothing in here. I can't find anything that I really want to wear. Nothing is really jumping out at me," I explain.

Ilesha states, "Bull shit! You know you got all

them damn clothes in your closet. Chick, you got clothes. I should come get something to wear out of your big ass closet! Every closet in your big ass house has clothes in it."

"I don't know what you are talking about," I say jokingly.

"I'm talking about that huge closet upstairs you got and the second master suite with the walk in closet. That's what I'm talking about," says Ilesha.

"Girl, you are crazy. Listen, do you wanna go to the mall, so we can get something to wear?" I ask.

"Yeah, that's cool. Come get me cause I'm not trying to drive out all of my gas," Ilesha says.

"Alright, I'll be there in a little bit," I reply.

I really don't feel like getting dressed in anything too fancy just to go to the mall, but I keep hearing the words of my mom and aunt echoing in my head.

"Care about your appearance. Don't leave the house looking any old kinda way. You never know who you may run into," they would say.

Those words are in the forefront of my mind as I rummage through my closet. It's very possible that I could meet someone while we're out and about shopping. I would hate to miss out on Mr. Right because I'm not dressed the part. I know it's not all about clothes, but first impressions go a long way. Since men are extremely attracted to physical attributes, I'm wearing an outfit that will entice them. Men lust before they love. I remember Sage told me that a while back before we began having conflicts.

"You can't get a job without a job interview," is what Sage would say all the time.

It's true. I know I won't be able to get a man if no one ever looks my way and approaches me. I have to ensure that someone tries to push up. Therefore, my outfit is alluring and my hair is tightened up nicely. No ponytails and sweats for me today. I went to the nail salon yesterday so my fingernails and toenails are freshly done as well. I am a man magnet. Somebody's son is going to see and want me today. I can feel it!

It's around 1pm when I pull up to Ilesha's house. Since I'm not going inside, I beep the horn for Ilesha to come to the car. She comes outside and is cleaner than freshly fallen snow. That's her norm. Ilesha is always dressed like she's about to walk the runway. When we were growing up in Linden, many people thought we were twins because we resemble one another and would always wear similar outfits.

When we were younger, my mom and her twin sister, Aunt Virginia, would often make comparisons between the two of them and Ilesha and me. They reported how their presence was always felt wherever they went much like Ilesha and me. On many occasions Ilesha and I would be mistaken for each other. We knew we looked a little bit alike, but never to the extent that other people made it seem. We definitely do have the likeness that my mom and Aunt Virginia have, even though they are identical twins. What's remarkable is that even through the years, they maintained the same weight, same style and are still inseparable. I really think that's why many people think Ilesha and I are twins. We have the same sense of fashion and are always together, along with Rachel, of course.

"Hey girl," I say as Ilesha gets into the car.

"Hey, it's nice as hell today!" says Ilesha.

I state, "It is. It's like 80 degrees. I called Rachel earlier to see if she wanted to go, but she couldn't get free. You know she already has her outfit together anyway."

Ilesha replies, "Yeah, I texted her earlier and she told me the same thing. What mall are you trying to go to?"

I say, "Let's go to Pentagon City. I wanna hit some of the stores out there."

"That's fine. I haven't been out there in forever. They used to have some real nice clothes. I hope that's still the case. That's where I bought my outfit for a New Year's party a few years ago," she replies.

We arrive at the mall and begin attacking the stores one by one. There are abundantly more stores in here since the last time we were here. The good thing is that there are more female clothing stores in here now, so we have plenty of options.

I ask Ilesha, "What kind of outfit are you looking for?"

"I'm looking for something tight that will show off my flat stomach and fat ass," she replies.

We both crack up laughing. Ilesha is absolutely serious though. She wants to show off all of the hard work she puts in at the gym. Unfortunately, my decision on what to wear is not so clear cut. I don't know if I want something tight and sexy to show off my curves. Racy could work, but it might send the wrong message. I could go with something elegant and sophisticated, but that outfit may make me seem like I'm boring. I'm open to whatever feels right. I hope I find something.

"Come on girl, let's go into Cinderella's. I keep hearing they have some stunning pieces in there," I say.

We walk into Cinderella's and are immediately greeted by the staff. The outfits and accessories they have are beautiful. It's almost like the designers of these clothes know exactly what I want. I could leave with all of this stuff. I went from not thinking I would be able to find anything at all, to not knowing exactly what to get. It's ironic how having options can make a decision extremely difficult. You would think it's simple to just pick one and keep it moving. The problem is when you have multiple options and can only choose one, you always feel like you are leaving something behind. Each option is better than the other for its respective reason. I keep looking and I find the perfect outfit! It tastefully combines the two looks I want. It's racy and tight yet still very elegant. I am good to go!

Ilesha says, "That outfit is gonna kill them tonight girl! Watch and see. As long as you don't stand next to me, you will be the center of attention."

I say, "Please, ain't nobody worried about you. I am about to kill it tonight whether you're beside me or not. Besides, you have a man. Just let me get mine. You better behave tonight."

Ilesha says, "I always behave when I have a man, although I may flirt a little."

I reply, "That's more than you should be doing."

"Girl please, a little flirting is harmless. All it does is spice things up a little bit. Throws a hint of intrigue into the mix. It keeps the blood pumping and life invigorating," Ilesha explains.

I told her to ask herself what Rachel would say to a comment like that. Rachel would disagree for sure. That would be too risqué for her. The thought of entertaining another man outside of her "bae" would be ludicrous to her and I agree. There is no need to entertain a man when you have another one waiting on you. It's not for me, but Ilesha doesn't feel that anything's wrong with it.

"To each his own," I say.

Still trying to prove her point, Ilesha states, "You have to admit, it's nice for a man to acknowledge and appreciate a nice looking woman. It doesn't have to go any further than that. Shit, it just reaffirms you still have it going on!"

We leave the mall and head back to Ilesha's house. Rachel meets us there, so we can do each other's eyebrows. Rachel is a whiz when it comes to doing eyebrows. She took cosmetology classes in high school and remains very skilled in the profession. Rachel does our eyebrows while we talk.

"So Rachel, what do you think about flirting with a guy while you are in a relationship?" I ask.

"Oh no! You know that's a no go! None of that extra stuff is allowed!" she exclaims.

Ilesha says, "Whatever. Don't nobody wanna hear all that!"

Rachel asks, "How would you feel if your dude was out there flirting with women in the streets? Wouldn't you would wanna beat him down?"

"I wouldn't want to beat him down. I would *definitely* beat his ass," Ilesha replies.

After we finish laughing at Ilesha's comments, we decide what time we are going to link back up for the all-white party. I also share with them the game plan for when we arrive. I know for a fact that there will be some guys who will come talk to me who I will not be interested in. Therefore, I came up with some signals just in case I need a rescue. I also put a few signals together in the event I want to talk to a guy alone. Hopefully, these tricks will help the night go smoothly. I don't have time to get stuck talking to a guy who I know I don't want. It seems like the guy you don't want talking to you is the one who will try to take up most of your time. I could be using that time to find my new love.

"This is going to be an interesting night. I can tell. We have signals and scams," Ilesha says.

Rachel says, "It is going be a very nice night. Girls' night out. I can't wait to get my two step on."

"I'm not trying to two step at all. I'm shaking my ass tonight," says Ilesha. "And I'm getting drunk."

"I'm only drinking socially. I can't go too heavy on the drinks. I have to make sure I'm on my 'A' game," I say.

"I think I'm going to drink water tonight. No adult beverages for me," says Rachel.

Ilesha replies, "Even better! I nominate you as our designated driver and you can drive my drunk ass home!"

Rachel and I look each other and just shake our heads. I leave Ilesha's house and drive to mine. I iron my clothes and get my accessories together. We all decide to wear red accessories with our outfits. I'm going to carry my MK bag and wear my MK shoes with a red and white MK scarf. I also have some yellow gold jewelry that

I'm going to wear to match the trim in my bag. I am ready for tonight. I sit all of my makeup out, so I can have everything in line when I start getting dressed. When it's time to go, I don't want to have to run around like a chicken with its head cut off. After I get my stuff together I take a nap, so I can be refreshed for tonight's festivities.

CHAPTER 3

Damn, that was a great nap. That was exactly what I needed. That power nap has me charged up and ready to go. I feel even better after taking a shower and brushing my teeth. I spent too much time in the shower and now I'm running a few minutes late. The hot water from the shower was feeling too good to just jump in and out. Plus, I barely get a chance to have long showers during the week, since I'm constantly on the go. Being a career oriented woman certainly has its pros and cons. I'm only a few minutes behind, so I should be fine. Rachel is picking Ilesha and me up since we plan to drink tonight. Rachel accepted Ilesha's abrupt offer to be the designated driver, which she doesn't mind. She'll also be the level headed one for the night. She has to keep us safe just in case there are some unsavory guys at the party. That's always how we roll. Whenever we go out, one of us is in charge of watching out for the others. For example, when my birthday came around last year, Ilesha was the one who didn't drink. It's hard to believe, but she didn't and she wouldn't let me or Rachel go overboard and look foolish either.

I have to admit, she played the part of being our bodyguard better than Kevin Costner did for Whitney Houston. That night could have potentially been the worst night of my life. I remember it like it was yesterday.

Me and the girls decided to celebrate my birthday at Club Love. The early part of my day went exactly as I planned. I slept in late to begin the day and then the girls and I linked up to do some shopping and eat dinner. After dinner, we parted ways so we could get ready to hit the club. Ilesha used some of her connects to get us on the VIP list, so we breezed past that long line and went directly into the club.

We had a private area, even though I actually like to interact with the crowd. Rachel and I were sipping on cocktails and dancing for the majority of the night. Ilesha was flirting with several men in the club, while also keeping an eye on us. Quite a few men approached us too, but we were more focused on us, so we really didn't pay them much attention. We turned down so many guys that we lost count. Most of them were very polite after we refused their advances, but a few were upset. Men don't take rejection very well. They'll also do anything to get what they want.

Two guys approached Rachel and me and asked to buy us drinks. We thought them buying us drinks was a bit cliché and they weren't the least bit creative with their approach. They were kind of cute and well put together, so we accepted the free drinks. After some light conversation and many fake laughs on our part, the guys asked us to go back to their respective places for some grownup activities. Men are so damn nasty; they will fuck anything with a hole. We had only been conversing for a half hour at most and they wanted us to go back to their places and give them our goods. Hell no! They had the wrong ones that night. They thought because they bought us a couple of drinks that they had earned some of our cookie.

Of course, we rejected their offer and they were not pleased with our decision. One guy even hinted that he wasted his time and money on us. Rachel and I realized that the situation was about to get tense, so we decided to go to the restroom to let the situation calm down. We really hoped they would realize they weren't getting any loving from us tonight and just move along. To our surprise, the two men stuck around and waited for us to return. When we came out of the restroom they were standing there with drinks for both of us.

One guy apologized for the insensitive comment his friend made pertaining to wasting his time. As a peace offering, they offered the drinks. We were at a point where we didn't want any more drinks, but we took them because we didn't want to be rude. The two guys walked away from us and went across the dance floor. They kept looking back at us as they walked away. We were puzzled as to why they were so interested in what we were doing, but just assumed they were just making sure we weren't still upset.

Ilesha walked up to us as the two men walked away. She had a slightly angry look on her face. Before we had a chance to say anything, she grabbed both of the drinks we were holding and threw them in the garbage. We didn't care that she dumped the drinks because we weren't going to drink them anyway, but we didn't want to be unappreciative of the guys' gesture. We couldn't throw the drinks away without them seeing us because they kept peering at us and scrutinizing every move we made. We figured she just didn't want us to drink anymore.

When she trashed the drinks, the two guys who bought them for us started heading back over. We could tell they were upset that the drinks had been thrown away. When they approached us, Ilesha started cursing them out and everyone in the immediate vicinity stopped to view what was going on. Rachel and I still didn't really know what was causing Ilesha's outrage. She quickly informed Rachel and me that she watched us the entire time we conversed with the two men.   Furthermore, she observed them putting a powdery substance in the drinks they presented to us as a peace offering.   It was probably the date rape drug.   Putting the date rape drug in an alcoholic beverage can have a potentially lethal impact on a person. At the very least, it could make a person pass out and be susceptible to whatever the perpetrator wants to do. They were upset because we didn't want to have sex with them, so they were going to rape us.

Rachel and I joined in on the tongue lashing. The two men didn't seem surprised at the unpleasant words we hurled at them. It had to be a very vile act because even Rachel was cursing at them. Rachel almost never uses foul language. I think the thought of getting violated touched her deeply. We eventually told them that we were calling the cops and they quickly cleared the area. Ilesha wanted to chase after them and fight, but Rachel and I told her not to worry about it. We didn't call the cops, but we did inform management in case they came back.   They should be aware of the scum they had in their establishment. We continued on with our night together and because of Ilesha we were spared from becoming rape victims. Needless to say, we haven't been back to that club and we're extremely cautious when accepting drinks from strangers.

The few minutes I'm behind will be negligible. There is no way they'll be here at eight because Rachel is picking up Ilesha first. Ilesha is never ready on time. I call Rachel to see how they are looking on time.

"Hey, are you already at Ilesha's house?" I ask.

"Yeah, I'm here now. She's almost ready. We should be there around eight fifteen," Rachel replies.

"Girl, I'm surprised that you'll be here that soon. You know how Ilesha does," I say.

"I know, right," Rachel replies.

We are both on the phone giggling when I hear Ilesha's voice in the background.

"I know you two are talking about me! It takes time to be as fine as me! Don't hate," screams Ilesha.

"Alright Rachel. I'll see you in a lil bit," I say.

The few extra minutes to get myself together are coming in handy. I like not having to rush with my makeup. Now, I'll have time to fix it if I mess up. I decide not to wear lipstick. My lips are plenty juicy and all I really need is some lip gloss to do the trick. I'm putting on some lip liner to really make my lips pop. It's eight fifteen and I hear a car pull into my driveway. Right after that, I receive a text from Rachel stating that they're here. I take one last look in the mirror to make sure my makeup is flawless, my outfit is looking good, and my booty is delicious. I go downstairs and we drive to the party.

There's no line, so we don't have to wait to enter. We give the man at the door our tickets and we walk right in. The room is beautifully decorated. There are white embellishments draped all around the room. The décor almost looks like a snow topped mountain because everything is a brilliant white. Even the DJ is dressed in all white attire.

There are three ballrooms and all of them are packed with people dressed in all white. Each of the ballrooms is playing a different type of music. One room is for contemporary music, another room is for old school music, and the third is catering to mostly reggae music. Everything seems well put together and we are looking forward to a fantastic time. Everyone has on their best clothes and is dressed exquisitely. The place smells like a perfume and cologne store because of all the varying fragrances in the air.

We are in the room that's playing contemporary music.

"This is my song! Let's go dance," I say.

Rachel and I hit the dance floor, but Ilesha goes to the bar to get a drink. Rachel and I are on the dance floor when two guys approach us.

"Can I get a dance?" one of the guys asks.

"Sure," I respond.

Rachel accepts an invitation to dance as well. We are all two stepping and then the guy twirls me around and moves in close to me. I don't mind that he's up on me. It's just dancing. Besides, it's been a while since I had a man this close and it's kind of nice. As he dances on me, I feel something poking me in my behind. I think to myself, I know this guy didn't get a hard on while we're dancing. I feel the poke once more and realize this guy's dick is hard. We haven't even been dancing for five minutes and here he goes. I'm feeling a little disgusted to have some strange guy's meat poking me and I wasn't even trying to put it on him.

In an attempt to not be rude, I dance forward a little bit hoping he won't slide up after me, but he does. Is this guy a weirdo or something? How could he get hard from dancing for just a few minutes? I have to stop dancing with him. I don't want to feel that again.

"Thanks for the dance. It was really nice of you, but I have to go find our other friend," I tell him.

Rachel follows me as I exit the dance floor to find Ilesha. Rachel didn't care that she ended her dance prematurely. She has a boyfriend and was only being my "wing woman". We walk up to the bar and Ilesha is just ordering her drink.

"Get me an amaretto sour. I need a drink after that dance," I say.

She orders the drinks for us and gets Rachel a bottle of water.

Rachel asks, "What happened that you got out

of dodge so quickly? You didn't think he was cute?"

Ilesha cuts in and says, "Yeah, I saw him. He's cute, girl!"

"He is cute, but he's nasty. He got a woody while we were dancing. That is a turn off!" I state.

Rachel says, "Eww, that is nasty. I would've stopped dancing with him too."

"That is some high school shit right there. A grown ass man with a hard dick from dancing? Something ain't right about that," Ilesha remarks while shaking her head.

"Well, you are killing that outfit girl. He was just turned on," says Rachel.

"Wait, I know what it is. Maybe he hasn't had sex in a long time like you!" says Ilesha.

I reply, "Now that's just wrong."

We get a good laugh and walk into another one of the ballrooms. The dance floor in this room is packed. Unfortunately, there are people walking through the center of the dance floor. I hate that. Someone always comes scooting past when you are in a groove. We decide not to head for the dance floor at all because there's an open spot right at the back of the party area. Me and my girls party like we're in college again. The music is without a doubt up to par and this second drink I'm sipping on is starting to loosen me up a bit. I am in a zone. We dance to four songs straight and then we finally go sit down.

"Girl, my legs are burning. I think I'm about to catch a cramp!" I say.

"That's what you get for trying to drop low to that Beyoncé song. Now your ass is paying for it," says Ilesha.

"I've been stretching everyday once we said we were coming," says Rachel.

"Me too, but I did drink a soda though. I should've been drinking water instead. I don't know what I was thinking," I say.

"Bump all that you talking. You're tired because you are old," says Ilesha.

I reply, "I may be old, but I'm sharper than most of these 21 year old women in here. I have a tight ass and stomach. Besides, if I'm old, you are too. We're the same damn age!"

We sit at the table for about fifteen minutes to recuperate as we people watch. I suggest we go stand by the bar because there aren't guys coming back to the seating area. I know I need to be visible in order to be approached. We are standing at the bar when this handsome man approaches us and singles me out. We made eye contact from across the room a couple of times, but I didn't expect him to come over to me. I love confidence in a man and he is definitely projecting it.

"Hello, my name is Marcus. And what is your name? Let me guess. Is it Angel or Precious?" he asks.

I feel his line is rather corny, but I appreciate

the compliment. I really don't need a man to approach me with pickup lines, but I am a bit flattered. I'm mostly flattered because he is so fine. His skin is unblemished and smooth as if he bathes in cocoa butter. I could gaze into his bedroom eyes for hours. I have to control myself.

I respond, "My name is Sheena. Thank you for the warm words. That's sweet."

"Thank you for being breath taking. Your beauty is unparalleled. When I spotted you from across the room, I knew I had to introduce myself," says Marcus.

"Oh, is that right? Why did you have to?" I ask.

He says, "If I hadn't, I would have regretted it and I would've been kicking myself for the rest of the night."

I'm glad he did come speak. He is very well groomed and articulate. Many men won't approach a woman if she's with other females because they feel they won't get a fair shot, but Marcus is fearless. His confidence is very attractive.

"Well, I'm glad you won't be kicking yourself tonight," I reply.

He replies, "Me too. I'm sure that would hurt badly."

"Oh okay. So you like to tell jokes. Marcus has a sense of humor. Laughter is therapy and I love to laugh," I say.

Marcus talks to me and the girls for about ten minutes and then offers to buy us drinks. Ilesha and I both order an amaretto sour and Rachel orders another bottle of water. He also orders himself a crown and coke. The conversation quickly went south when Marcus reaches into his pocket to pay for the drinks. He pulls out a large wad of money. He is clearly trying to impress us by making it so visible.

I don't mind him flaunting his cash. If he wants to spend money to impress me, that's fine by me. Unfortunately, he makes a huge mistake when he pulls the money out of his pocket. This man or should I say asshole, inadvertently drops his wedding band. He tries to act like he didn't drop anything, but we all see it. Rachel and Ilesha become very interested in his next move. Marcus places his foot over the ring to try to conceal it and then drops a dollar, so he can pretend he's bending down to pick up the money. It'll take some A+ acting skills to try to get that over on all three of us and Marcus is not an A+ actor. He tries to slide the ring back into his pocket, but Ilesha comments on his blunder before I do.

"Get ya snake ass out of here! I can't believe you. You are the worst!" Ilesha yells.

You would think Ilesha is in a relationship with Marcus. She is irate and cursing him out. Why does it always seem like some fool causes us to make a scene? Rachel is calm like always and not saying much.

"That's not nice. It would be best if you leave us alone. Thank you for buying the drinks. Enjoy your night," Rachel says.

I'm not mad, just a little disappointed. I should have known that a guy as silky smooth as he is would be taken. I'm so happy that he dropped that ring because if he hadn't I could have gotten played. I've potentially been saved from a lot of hurt. At some point, I would have given him my energy, time, and body only to find out he's married. That would have caused me a lot of pain and anguish. Men are so conniving. How could he do this to his wife? I have some words for Marcus too.

"You are a loser. If I knew your wife, I would tell her exactly what you are up to!" I say firmly. "You don't deserve a good woman!"

"You ain't nothing but a jump off anyway. You ain't even worth a fuck. It's not that damn serious," Marcus says.

As Marcus walks away Ilesha gives him a parting gift. She splashes him with the amaretto sour he purchased. I think she would have hit him if Rachel and I weren't blocking her path.

"Girl, you should have slapped him right in his damn face! How he gonna say that shit after what he tried to do? I don't like that. That just doesn't sit well with me. He can't get that," says Ilesha as she moves her head from side to side and makes gestures with her hands.

Rachel states, "Don't let him mess up our

night. He clearly isn't worth it. We should just brush it off and move on. Not all men are like him Sheena. Don't be discouraged."

I'm not discouraged. The night is still young and there are many nice looking guys in here. Besides, we are having a great time regardless of that fool. I'm more upset that Ilesha squandered her drink instead of drinking it.

"Thanks for having my back girls, but next time keep your drink. No need to waste your drink on a waste of a man," I say.

Rachel says, "We always got your back. Let's hit the lobby. They have a picture booth set up out there. You know we need one for the album. I know we've taken several pictures with our phones already, but to me it's not the same."

We leave the bar area and walk to the lobby where the pictures are being taken. The line is long and I don't want to wait, but Rachel is intent on getting a professional picture of the trio. Ilesha is all for it too. She wants the picture because she knows she's looking good and Rachel wants the picture for sentimental reasons.

While we're waiting on the picture line, another guy approaches me. He's extremely fine. He's much better looking than that trifling asshole Marcus.

"Hi, my name is Kevin. And you are?" he asks.

"Hello Kevin, my name is Sheena," I respond.

"It's nice to make your acquaintance," Kevin

replies.

I ask, "What brings you out tonight?"

"Me and my boys used to come to the all-white parties back in the day. It's been a couple years since we last came, but thought it might be fun," says Kevin.

"That's funny. That's the same situation as me and my girls. We're just trying to have a nice night out," I say.

Kevin seems to be a pretty nice guy. I'm at least enjoying his company. We take a picture together after me and the girls do. As we chat, I gently move my hair behind my right ear as my signal to the girls that I would like some alone time with Kevin. Ilesha and Rachel excuse themselves to the bar and Ilesha threatens Kevin not to try to take advantage of me because she'll be watching. They won't venture off very far and will lay eyes on me periodically in the event things go awry and I need intervention. Kevin seems sweet and doesn't appear to have any hidden agendas. He and I enjoy a lengthy conversation as he tells me that he's a lawyer who works for a company that has interests in Dubai. He is very poised and professional. If first impressions mean anything, this guy is perfect. I'm really intrigued by him.

"Do you travel to Dubai often for work?" I ask.

"Yes, I'm often out of the country. Sometimes I'm gone for weeks at a time. I love my career, but sometimes the airports and hotels can be a bit overwhelming," he explains.

I was hoping he would say that he's rarely out of the country, but my luck isn't that good. Maybe it's just not meant to be. I'm not interested in a long distance relationship even if the guy was in the United States, but I'm certainly not down with a relationship where my man is never in the country. That defeats the purpose of having a man. I want my man to be home regularly, so I can be with him and have him hold me in his arms.

"I feel you on the traveling all the time. It can absolutely be overwhelming. Most people who don't travel admire it not knowing how much work it really is. I feel like you and I are kindred spirits," I say.

"I feel the same way. What are you doing tonight after the party ends?" asks Kevin.

"Me and my girls are going home. We may grab a bite to eat beforehand if they want. Why do you ask?" I inquire.

Kevin replies, "I don't want to seem too forward, but I don't want our night to end. Maybe you can come home with me or me with you? I would love to wake up next to a beautiful woman, such as you."

I don't know if I should be mad or flattered. He is basically asking me to spend the night with him and have sex. Even though he asked in a nice way, it's still the same message. He wants to fuck me. Every man expects you to have sex with him if you spend the night. I don't want our night to end either, but I am not having sex with him on the first night. I don't know him like that. Besides like I said before, people are crazy. I don't need him knowing where I live. He might be a psycho or something.

"Kevin, I don't think it's the best idea for us to spend the night together, but let's get up tomorrow for brunch," I reply.

"I understand your position about spending the night. However, brunch won't work for tomorrow because I fly overseas tomorrow afternoon," Kevin explains.

Kevin and I talk a little while longer. We exchange phone numbers and agree to keep in contact with one another. Kevin leaves the party and I go find Rachel and Ilesha. We dance to one more song before we depart the party.

"Girl, you shoulda got you some of him. Once he met you, he didn't pay anybody else any attention and there were other good looking women in there besides us," says Ilesha.

Rachel says in disagreement, "You did the right thing. You didn't want to send the wrong message by sleeping with him. He could be a grease ball like that guy Marcus."

"He did seem really nice, but he can't get some of me just off of a few minutes of talking. If it's meant to be, we'll link back up in the future. I have his contact information, so it's cool," I say.

We exchange stories about what happened tonight as we drive home. Rachel drops me off first because my house is closer.

"Thanks for coming out tonight. I really needed to get out. Text me when you get in safely. Later," I say.

"Bye girl," they both say.

I close the car door and walk to the house. They watch me enter and then they drive off. It's about thirty minutes later and my phone chimes alerting me to the arrival of a message. It's Rachel letting me know she has dropped Ilesha off and she's home. After I read the text, I go to bed.

CHAPTER 4

I am two months into my search for a potential mate. Unfortunately, I'm no closer to having a new man than I was two months ago when I first started looking. The only male communication I'm receiving is from Kevin, but that's pointless because he's never around. He keeps in contact regularly as he said he would and I thoroughly enjoy our conversations. I really wish he didn't travel so much. I feel like we have a lot in common. Anyway, he's not here, so it's a moot point. I don't know what the problem is. It's not like I haven't been trying to meet guys. The girls and I have been some of everywhere. We've been to parties, clubs, church, and poetry nights just to name a few. I'm spending a lot of money keeping myself looking good. I can say the money I'm spending on my fitness club membership is really paying off though. I feel and look better than normal. I've even dropped a full dress size without losing my booty.

I didn't think finding the right man would be easy, but I certainly didn't think it would be this difficult. This is a very intense process. Every time I want to give up my search and indulge in an entire bucket of ice cream, I think about what my mom used to tell me whenever I wanted to rush through college and start my career.

"Good things come to those who wait," mom would say.

That was her way of telling me to be patient and not to rush things. She would explain that I will appreciate something more if it doesn't come easily. She was right because all of the things that were toilsome to achieve, I hold them dear to my heart. Even though I know that patience is a virtue, I still want a man now. The more I want a man, the more I'm willing to take a chance on someone I know I shouldn't take a chance on. I find myself making excuse after excuse for the guys who approach me.

"I can teach him how to dress. He isn't that much overweight. So what he smokes and plays video games all day," I would say to my girls.

They keep me grounded and focused on the real goal. I can't take a consolation prize for the man I want. Why should I settle? I haven't settled on anything I ever wanted out of life and I am not going to settle now. I'll just be patient and keep looking.

It's finally Friday and it's been a long week. With the nonstop meetings, working overtime and teaching class, I don't know how I survived. I'm tired tonight, to say the least, so I am not leaving the house. I'm looking forward to just relaxing in the house by myself. Some "me" time is all I need right now. As I head to the linen closet to grab my blanket and nestle on the couch, my phone begins to ring. Who could this be calling me? Oh, it's just Ilesha.

"Hey girl. What you up to?" Ilesha asks.

"Hey, I'm sitting in the house about to watch some television and just relax. Why? What you doing tonight?" I ask.

Ilesha replies, "Rachel said she wants to go bowling. I told her I would go. You gotta come too."

I reply, "Girl, I already told myself that I'm staying in tonight. I really don't feel like going out, plus my period is on. I don't feel like myself."

"Umm too bad! You've been dragging me and Rachel some of everywhere lately and we didn't falter one bit, so now it's your turn," Ilesha snaps back.

She has a point. I have been running them to death. Not to mention they've been spending their hard earned money hanging out with me. I really don't want to go, but it's only fair. We always make sacrifices for one another. Today is my day to suck it up.

"Okay, okay. What bowling alley are you going to?" I ask.

I pull myself together mentally and prepare for a night out that I really don't want. I told Ilesha that I would go, but I didn't say I was getting dressed up. Besides it's only bowling. It's not like I need to put on my best outfit to throw a hard ball around. I'm putting on an outfit that's cute for the occasion and I'm not wearing any makeup either. My lip gloss and perfume will be just fine. I hope we don't bowl for long. I want to be back in my bed as early as possible. I can wear my hair in a ponytail and throw on my hat. It does match my outfit. This is my "bumming it" outfit in my opinion, but it's cute to many people.

I drive to the bowling alley. It takes me almost ten minutes to find a parking space. This bowling alley is packed. There are people everywhere. As I enter, I see Rachel and Ilesha at a lane putting on their shoes, so I walk over to them. We exchange greetings to one another and then engage in regular conversation.

Rachel says, "I haven't been bowling in a long time. I'm glad you came out tonight. We're gonna have fun."

"You won't have fun once I start beating the nipples off your tits. You know you can't out bowl me," says Ilesha.

"Whatever! I haven't lost a game of bowling to you two since we were in college, so I don't see why I should start losing now. This game is mine!" I say.

"Well, I just hope to be competitive. I want to bowl at least 115. This is all just for kicks. It's not like we're joining a bowling league," says Rachel.

"This is a new day. I have been bowling a lot with my man lately and I'm a whole lot better than before," explains Ilesha.

Rachel has some coupons to get us a discount on the games we bowl. She's always been the frugal type. Rachel can find a coupon for just about anything. Her philosophy is "why pay full price if you don't have to?" I can't argue with that. With her coupon, we get each our games at half price. I lost one of the games we played, but I won two. This fourth game is very close and there are only a few frames to go. Ilesha is trash talking like usual, even though she's bowled several gutter balls. Rachel ended up halfway down the lane when her fingers got stuck in the bowling ball. I almost took out a group of people behind us when my bowling ball slipped out of my hand, while I was swinging back preparing for my release. Luckily, no one was injured (only my pride momentarily). I am having a great time because I'm winning and because we can't stop laughing. Even the pizza in this bowling alley is delicious. I accidentally spill Ilesha's soda, so I go to the concession stand to buy her another one.

It's fortuitous that I spilled her drink. I am in

line to replace her soda when a guy walks past me. He is fine! I can tell he works out regularly because his chest is standing up and sticking out. He looks like a body builder. His shoulders are very broad and he's every bit of six feet tall. I'm pretending to look off into space, so it's not so obvious that I'm really looking at him. I can see him out of my peripheral vision as he floats by. This man is beautiful. As he passes, I turn back to analyze the menu board to see how much Ilesha's drink is going to cost me. A moment later, I hear a voice make a comment about someone's perfume. I look over my shoulder and see this jaw-dropping man looking back at me.

"Excuse me young lady. If you don't mind me asking, what fragrance are you wearing? The pleasant smell grabbed me as I walked past, so I have to ask," he explains.

"My perfume is called Flower Bomb. Is it too strong?" I ask.

"No, not at all. It's one of the most delightful scents I have ever smelled in my life. There's nothing like a beautiful woman who smells good," he says.

"Beautiful! Oh, so you're calling me beautiful?" I ask.

"Yes, I am. My name is Eric. I just call it how I see it," he says. "You could steal the wind out of a tornado."

I am blushing now for sure. I hope he can't tell. I don't want to appear to be completely enamored by his slick tongue. He doesn't know that I'm witty and have a pretty slick tongue myself.

"Well, thank you. You are too kind. I'm glad to meet someone who clearly takes care of his body," I say.

I can't stop staring at his herculean body. His shoulders and arms are perfectly chiseled as if Michelangelo created this masterpiece himself. I can tell there's even more of a treat nicely tucked underneath the Polo shirt he's wearing. I wouldn't mind running my hands over each and every defined ripple in his torso.

"A lot of hard work. It looks like someone is taking care of your body too. You must watch what you eat and workout regularly," Eric says.

I wish he would take care of my body. *Grab me and kiss me right now!* Those are the thoughts going through my mind. I'm going to wait for him to ask me for my number or some contact information. I don't want to miss out on him, but I don't want him to think I'm thirsty for a man either.

"Yes, I have a lil gym membership. Just trying not to fall off. It's nothing major though. Oh my goodness, I forgot my girls are waiting for me. It's probably my turn to bowl. Let me get back," I say.

"Oh, my bad. I didn't mean to hold you up. I didn't catch your name," Eric says.

I reply, "I am so sorry. Where are my

manners? I'm Sheena. It's nice to meet you. Even though you are the reason I didn't get my drink," I articulate. I wink and say, "Just kidding."

"Nice meeting you as well, funny lady. Get back to your girls and your game. If you like, I'll grab your drink and bring it over to you," Eric says.

I accept his offer and tell him what type of drink to order and the lane we are in. I wonder if I should give him the money for the drink. It's only a couple of dollars, but I don't want him to think I need him to buy me a drink or that I'm trying to use him. On the other hand, he did offer. If he's a gentleman, he will pay for it. Sometimes, a gesture goes a long way.

"We are on lane ten. Come on over, but I must warn you that I'm with two of my girlfriends. They are harmless though. Well, at least one of them is. I'll be waiting for my drink," I say.

I walk back to our lane and let the girls know that Eric will be coming over to hang with us for a little bit. I also tell them not to ask him a million questions. I know Rachel won't, but Ilesha will be all over him. Eric approaches us with the drink. He even has drinks for Ilesha and Rachel. Too bad we're not going to drink them. We've learned our lesson.

"Sheena, here is your drink. I didn't know if your friends were thirsty or not, so I bought them something to drink as well," Eric narrates.

"That was very nice of you," I say.

I introduce Eric to Rachel and Ilesha. As soon as the introductions are complete, Ilesha does what she does best.

"Ya name is Eric, right? So Mr. Eric, are you married? How many baby mommas you got?" Ilesha asks.

I want to apologize, but he doesn't even flinch. He answers her questions without hesitation. He is smoother than Bill Clinton with his responses. I'm mesmerized by his calmness.

"You don't have to answer her questions. She is one tough cookie. If you can withstand her, you can withstand anybody," I say.

"No, she is light work. I can handle her. She can't be as bad as my students' parents. They are a force to be reckoned with," Eric replies.

"Oh okay. Are you a school teacher?" Rachel asks.

Eric says, "No, I used to be. I'm a high school principal."

Ilesha screams, "Damn! That means you're making good money. Baller in the building!"

Leave it to Ilesha to put someone on the spot. Eric seems to be confident and pretty flexible. He doesn't take offense to Ilesha counting his pockets. He's just rolling with the punches. Eric is here with some high school students who are in a club that he sponsors at the school. It speaks volumes about someone who gives up his or her personal time for others. Eric talks to us for a few more minutes and then asks me to take a walk with him.

"Thanks for taking time out of your night to talk to me," he says.

"It's cool. I enjoyed your company. Again, thanks for the drinks. I really appreciate it," I say.

Eric says, "You should repay me by allowing me to whoop you in a game of bowling sometime soon."

I retort, "You will lose miserably. I have skills. Is this your way of asking me for my number and a date all in one?"

"Yes, it is. I hope it's gonna work," he replies.

I give Eric my number and he tells me to expect to hear from him very soon. I hope he calls because he seems to be a good catch. He cares about kids and he is a professional. Not to mention, he's out of this world handsome. He's winning with me already. I walk back to our lane and Rachel and Ilesha start picking with me.

Rachel says, "I hear wedding bells."

Ilesha counters, "I hear the headboard banging up against the damn wall like thunder. You think his package is big? He got some big ass hands and feet, so you know his dick is big too. That's where the rule of threes comes from. Hands, feet, dick!"

Rachel says, "Girl, you are just nasty and freaky."

"Don't act like I'm the crazy one. The only

thing better than a handsome man is a handsome man with a hefty bank account and a long thick dick," says Ilesha.

"I do like them thick and long. More importantly he has to know what to do with it," I say.

Rachel says, "I agree, but you two are just so vulgar with yours. A lady is supposed to be discreet. You can't just be broadcasting the business."

"He is a whole lot of man! I hope it works out," says Ilesha.

We talk about Eric and their boyfriends too. They already have me and Eric married with kids. I'm open to whatever because you never know what lies ahead. I'll just play it by ear. We bowl one more game and I win. After the game, we talk a little more as we leave the bowling alley.

"Now aren't you glad you came out tonight?" Rachel asks.

"Yeah, she is. Talking about she wanted to stay in and relax. Hell no girl! Ain't no relaxing when you going after something you claim you want. You gotta get your tail up and go get it," says Ilesha.

"Heck yeah, I'm glad I came out. Eric is super fiiiine!!! Alright ladies, I'm going home. Talk to you later," I state.

CHAPTER 5

It's a month since I met Eric. He and I are communicating pretty regularly. He either texts me or dials me up for a brief good morning conversation. He's also brought lunch to me at work three times. He's bringing me lunch today too. He's a perfect gentleman. Eric is a sweetheart. I love the fact the he's very considerate of my time, feelings, and beliefs. This man is sensitive, but not too soft or weak. He's going out of his way to keep me happy and show me that he is for real.

I told him a few days ago that I didn't want to have sex with him because I feel it's too soon. It didn't seem to bother him as he didn't even wince. In fact, that day he brought me flowers and took me to dinner. He informed me that naturally he wants to have sex with me, but only when I'm comfortable. He's putting no pressure on me to have sex with him. Everything is free flowing and fun. In a backwards sort of way, him not pressuring me for sex is making me want to give him some. I wouldn't mind pouncing on him and riding his surfboard. I can tell he's holding a pretty nice package. It's difficult for him to conceal it in his khakis and slacks.

I'm not going to give in though. It's too early to let him get some. I'll use this time to evaluate him and see what he's all about. I am the prize and he is on my time. It's not like I'm forcing him to pursue me. We're not even officially in a relationship. He is free to talk to anyone he wants to talk to and I am free to kick it with whomever I desire. It just so happens that he is completely focused on me. He is the only man I communicate with on a daily basis. I am still talking to Kevin fairly frequently when he gets a free moment from all of his world traveling. We also text to check in with one another. Kevin is a real cool dude.

Eric walks into my place of employment with my lunch and a single long stemmed rose. All of the ladies at the job are jealous of me. I'm sure they're jealous because Eric is handsome, well-spoken, and in great shape. He's also considerate enough to bring me lunch and a flower to my job. I would probably be jealous if he wasn't here for me. I love the attention he's giving me; I almost feel like I have a man.

"A single rose and food for the queen," Eric

says as he bows before me.

"Thank you my knight. That's so sweet of you. The rose is beautiful. You didn't have to," I reply.

"I know I didn't, but I wanted to see your face light up like it is now. You would think that you don't get flowers often," Eric states.

I inform him that as shocking as it may seem, I don't get flowers often. The last person to buy flowers for me was Sage and that was forever ago. Only those flowers didn't mean a thing because Sage was playing me the whole time we were together.

As I look at the rose and smell its wonderful fragrance, I'm filled with emotion. I don't know why, it is just a rose. My hormones are on ten and I guess it's just one of those days that if I saw a cat snuggle with a dog I might cry. I try to conceal this crazy moment I'm having, but I'm unsuccessful. With no control over my actions, I give Eric a giant hug. I'm not talking about a church hug where there's a foot of space between us either. I'm referring to the type of embrace that places my private part perfectly aligned with his. My suspicion of him being well endowed is confirmed. As we hug, I feel a huge knot tucked between his legs.

I can't deny that feeling his arms wrapped around me has gotten me slightly turned on. There's no telling what would happen right now if we were clasped together like this somewhere besides my office. Hell, maybe if we were already having sex, I would let him get a quickie right here. A midday tryst has never hurt anyone, unless they got caught. One moment I'm thinking how glad I am we're in this office and the next moment I'm wishing we were at my house with full privacy.

The smell of his cologne is summoning sexual desires out of me that I've been trying to suppress. I find myself slightly gyrating on his package. I hope he doesn't notice. I just miss this feeling so much that my body is acting separately from my mind. My body wants me to pull down his pants and ride his pony. Actually, it feels more like a full grown bull than a pony.

While we hug, Eric reaches down and squeezes my lower back. I love his strong hands groping my body. My wish right now is that he continues down the small of back and grabs my ass forcefully. I know my body and I'm sure my kitty cat would gush with moisture if he does that. Let's just say, I can't be held responsible for what would transpire if it reaches that point. I'm certain my body would overpower any voice of reason and he would get the goods right here, right now.

Instead of grabbing my booty, he runs his hands in the other direction. Eric slides his hands up my back and runs his fingers through my hair. I guess I should have known that he's too much of a gentleman to be so brazen to grab my behind without at least a hint of prior approval. To my surprise, him running his hands up my back and fingers through my hair have an arousing effect on me. The way he's touching me is very sensual.

I know it's been a long time since I've had sex, but I remember enough about it to know that a long kiss is forthcoming. I lift my head from nearly resting on his shoulder, so I can get in kissing position. His mouth is definitely one I want to feel on me. I hope he can kiss. If he's a lousy kisser, it will kill the vibe for sure.

Eric switches from rubbing his fingers through my hair to slowly rubbing his hand down my shoulder and arm until he stops at my hand and holds it. He raises my hand up to his face and gives me a soft kiss with his succulent lips on the backside of my hand. After he kisses my hand, he looks me in the eyes and starts talking. I have to admit that I'm slightly disappointed, but I know this isn't the time or place.

I place the flower in water and Eric and I eat lunch in my office while we chat. Eric is quite the conversationalist. He asks the questions that make you think deeply. It's never quiet when we are together. I feel like we can converse about anything.

"Don't you have a school to run?" I ask.

He replies, "Yes, I do, but I made time to see you for a moment. I'm leaving now, but enjoy the rest of your day. Call me later."

I say, "No, you should call me. Maybe you can

stop by the house if you get a minute this evening."

Since I haven't invited him to my home before, I know he's probably thinking he's going to get some loving. Maybe, maybe not. We'll see. I feel comfortable enough now to invite him to my home. He hasn't displayed any signs of crazy thus far.

"That sounds good. I'll give you a call. I have a staff meeting at the end of the day, but after that I'm free," Eric says.

He leaves and I finish the rest of my lunch. I am super hungry, but I didn't want him to see me devour the food. He doesn't ever need to see me eat like a piranha. My mom taught me to never let a man see me not at my best. I keep a clean house, but I make sure it's extra clean if I'm having male company. I hope Eric is able to come by later. I really enjoy his company. His cologne smells awesome and it makes me want to be on him. The scent is light, but masculine. I love it.

Things are under control at work today, so I leave early and head to the house. I'm getting things situated just in case Eric is able to come over. I also want to freshen myself up before he arrives. I'm making some baked chicken, mashed potatoes, and mixed vegetables for dinner. I'll make enough for two servings. If he comes by, he can eat with me and if not, I'll have lunch for tomorrow. Either way I'm covered. Men like when women cater to their needs.

It's now five thirty. I take the chicken out of the oven and my phone starts ringing. It's Eric. He's on his way over here to visit for a while. I'm glad that I didn't have to call him. I don't want him to think that I'm overbearing. My doorbell rings at six o'clock.

I ask, "Who is it?"

"It's Eric," he says.

"Here I come," I reply as I take a quick glance at myself in the mirror.

When I open the door Eric's cologne floats smoothly into my nostrils and infiltrates my body. His cologne is like an aphrodisiac. Just from the smell of it, my tunnel of love is responding and going crazy. This is not good. I should not be this turned on without him even touching me. I know he wore this cologne on purpose. I hope he hugs me.

"Good evening beautiful. Something sure smells good and so does the food," Eric states as he walks into the living room.

He walks over to me and gives me a nice strong hug. I don't want to let go, even more, I don't want him to let me go. His body feels like a warm blanket freshly out of the dryer and he smells sooooooo good. He kisses me on my cheek as a part of his greeting and I slowly step back to respond.

I reply, "Thanks, I'm making dinner. You can have some if you choose. My perfume is made by Tory Burch, in case you're wondering."

"After smelling that, I just want to eat it all up," Eric says.

I wonder if he's talking about eating my dinner or if he is talking about eating me. I'm actually hoping he's referring to the latter. I could really go for some tongue action on my sweet spot. He just doesn't know the eruption he would get if he ate me. His mouth and lips are something out of this world. He probably doesn't even go down. I need to focus on him and stop fantasizing.

"You're hungry, huh? Well, I'll make you a plate. Dinner will be ready in about ten minutes," I say.

Eric and I eat dinner and have a deep conversation. He tells me about his opinions on various topics such as abortion, cheating, politics, and a myriad of other things. I don't agree with all of his viewpoints, but I do enjoy listening to him. He is a very skilled speaker. I love the way words flow off of his lips.

We are now sitting on the couch listening to music while sipping on some wine. The wine has about fifty percent control of my body. If he makes a move, I may be done for. As luck would have it, a slow song comes on the radio and Eric asks me to dance. I accept his request and we dance in my living room.

"You are pretty light on your feet. It's almost like you are hovering, not dancing," I remark.

"Well, when you have a beautiful woman in

your arms it's easy to be on cloud nine. It's like gravity doesn't exist," Eric comments.

"You have a line for everything I see. Such a slick tongue!" I say.

Eric asks, "You wanna see how slick it is?"

Before I have a chance to respond, Eric kisses me. The kiss is exactly what I need. He's also pulling me close and I can feel his big hands squeezing my soft booty. I start grinding on him while we kiss hoping I can feel some sensation on my clit. As sensitive as my coochie is, I may be able to cum if I'm lucky. I have one leg planted firmly and the other is making its way up and down his leg. I can tell Eric is aroused because he's breathing heavy and grabbing me even tighter. He's hands are seemingly all over my body. He grips the base of my neck and a new sensation goes through my body. I'm in trouble.

I start to tell him that I want him to throw me down on the couch and give me a good pounding, but I catch myself. Instead, I reluctantly end the kiss. I let him know that I enjoyed the kiss, but it's late and he has to go. Part of me wants him to stay and see what the bulge in his pants amounts to, but the other side knows he doesn't deserve to have my body just yet. I can't share it with everybody.

"I look forward to spending more time with you," Eric says.

I reply, "The feeling is mutual."

"Dinner was delicious. I'll cook for you next

time if that's okay with you," Eric states.

"Oh, you cook? I would love for you to cook for me. Consider it a date. Have a good night and thanks for coming," I say.

I escort Eric to the door and he leaves for the night.

CHAPTER 6

Ilesha is taking her sweet ole time coming out of the house. She knows Rachel is always on time and will be waiting for us at the restaurant. Let me call Rachel and let her know we are going to be a few minutes late. When I grab my phone, a picture of a world map is flashing on the screen. The world map is the picture I use to come through when Kevin is calling me, since he's always on the go. I'm glad I went to get my phone because the ringer is off and I would've missed the call.

"Hey, Kevin. How are you Mr. International?" I ask.

"I'm great! Back in town. Figured I would hit you up," Kevin says.

"Oh yeah, you did say you would be in town this weekend," I say.

"Sure did. When I face timed you the other

day, you said you would be available. Are you still trying to hang out?" he asks.

Ilesha comes out the house and gets in the car as I talk to Kevin. She assumes that I'm talking to Eric and almost puts me under the gun.

She says, "Tell Eric I said hello."

I am so glad he didn't hear her. I know how loud Ilesha is, so luckily I thought to put the phone on mute as she was getting in the car. I really didn't want to have to explain that. Even though I'm not obligated to anyone, it still isn't a topic I want to discuss. Kevin is real laid back and is a nice guy, but his work schedule is too hectic for me. He is relationship material otherwise.

"Of course, I'm still down to hang out. When and what do you have in mind?" I ask.

"We can grab some dinner tomorrow night if you're free. Catch up face to face instead of via computer and phone," Kevin says.

"That works for me! Well, text me where and what time. I have my bestie in the car and I don't want to be rude," I say.

Kevin texts me where and when he wants to link up tomorrow night for dinner. I haven't seen him since we first met at the all-white party, but he keeps in contact as promised. I love when a man keeps his word. I like knowing he wasn't bullshitting me the night we met. There was definitely an attraction between us that night and I'm looking forward to seeing him again.

We arrive at the restaurant and of course Rachel is already inside.

"Ilesha is the reason we are late," I say immediately.

Ilesha replies, "She's right, but I'm always late, sometimes."

We all start laughing at the foolishness of Ilesha's statement.

Ilesha explains, "Now I may be part of the reason we're late, but we would've been here sooner if somebody wasn't distracted on the phone."

"Rachel, I wasn't distracted. Kevin called and we spoke briefly. Clearly, I was not distracted. We have a date for tomorrow," I say.

When I say that I have a date with Kevin to Rachel, she and Ilesha look at one another quickly. I don't know why.

"Clearly distracted," say Ilesha and Rachel in unison.

"I am not. I am on point," I shoot back.

Rachel asks, "You mean to tell us that you meant to schedule Eric and Kevin for a date on the same night? Remember you and Eric are supposed to be going to dinner too."

"Oh my goodness! I totally forgot about that. When Kevin said he's in town, my mind went blank. Shoot! What am I going to do?" I ask.

"It's simple, you haven't seen Kevin in months plus he's only around occasionally, so hang out with him. You see Eric all the time," says Ilesha.

Rachel says, "I agree with what she said. It only makes sense. Eric will understand. Just cancel."

Rachel is the one who gives sound advice. If she says it's a good idea, then it has to be. Her mindset is programmed on diplomacy at all times. She always sees the least abrasive way of getting a goal accomplished. I've never canceled on Eric in the past, so this will be a first. I don't want to lie, so I won't offer a reason for canceling.

"You are doing it big! You went from no dates to two dates with fine ass men!" exclaims Ilesha.

Rachel jokingly says, "I'm jealous. You are pulling them left and right."

They ride me hard while we eat dinner. They are quite comical. I guess I deserve the jokes because I made such a big deal over not having anyone.

"So how is Eric treating you?" Rachel asks.

"Everything is good. He is such a great listener. He listens to my problems and thoughts and doesn't try to fix them when I just need him to listen. He's a great catch," I say.

I decide to take their advice and cancel my plans with Eric, so I can hang with Kevin. Kevin wants me to meet him at Ruth's Chris Restaurant. That place is expensive, but the food sure is delicious. I haven't eaten there since I graduated from college. I remember I selected the stuffed chicken and I was full beyond belief. I will never forget the high bill that came, but it was worth it. The service and food were impeccable.

I guess Kevin wants to woo me by taking me to such an expensive place. It's only our first date and he is going all out. Well, I'm not sure if I can even call it a first date. It may be more like two friends getting together for dinner. Either way, it is still an expensive first outing. If we become a couple in the future, I wonder how he will top this.

Look at me. I'm a mess. I haven't even been out with Kevin and I'm already talking about us possibly being a couple. I've played the scenario in my head several times. I can picture Kevin and me together, but I can also envision Eric and me as one. I don't even know if either one of them wants me beyond having sex. What I do know is that they at least want some of this. All men want to have sex if their tools work properly.

I know exactly what outfit to wear. This outfit shows all of my curves, but is still slightly conservative. It's the type of outfit to get a guy's motor running, but not tell all of my business. He is definitely going to be intrigued by my ensemble. Not to mention, my curls are freshly done. He will not know what hit him.

I'm excited about meeting up again. I've enjoyed our correspondences since we first met. I often think back to our first meeting and how tempted I was to go home with him. I've never had a one night stand or even considered it until I met him. He is so smooth and sexy. I feel secure with him because he's so strong and manly. His words through texting and talking have a calming and reassuring tone. There's absolutely no panic in his voice.

I arrive at the restaurant at 7 o'clock sharp. I valet park because I don't want to walk through the parking lot. I want to make sure my perfume is the first thing he smells. I wonder what kind of car he drives. With all of the traveling he does, he probably makes a lot of money and drives a luxury vehicle. On the other hand, he travels so much that he doesn't need to drive an expensive car. It would be pointless and a waste of money.

Kevin is already in the lobby waiting for me. I'm glad he's on time because I loathe waiting and I find it extremely inconsiderate when a person is late. A man who is punctual is such a turn on. It says a lot about his personality. It signifies he's stable and in control of things. The way he's looking right now I wish he was in control of my body bent over, while he penetrates me from behind. After Kevin and I greet one another, he pays me a compliment.

Kevin says, "I should call the cops on you."

In a confused tone, I ask, "Why would you call the cops on me? What have I done?"

"Your beauty has stolen my breath from me," Kevin replies.

He makes the comment in such a serious tone that I almost believe that I've stolen his breath from him. He didn't even crack a smile after he said that.

"Your words are flattering. I can't take too much of your kindness. It isn't every day I hear words like that when referring to me. Thank you," I say.

We follow the hostess to our table and sit down. Kevin and I talk about current events and the conversation is flowing smoothly. The waiter brings us our drinks and is holding an iris. The iris is my favorite flower. The waiter sits our drinks down as well as the iris. I am sitting here in amazement.

I ask, "Kevin, how did you know that the iris is my favorite flower? I absolutely love them. It's beautiful!"

His response is commensurate with his personality.

"The flower is beautiful, but pales in comparison to your beauty. Lucky guess on my part," Kevin replies.

I'm flattered by the flower. I know I've never once told him about how I love this flower, so I'm bewildered as to how he knows. This man is mysterious and dark, and I am smitten by it. What I like even more is that he is acting like the flower isn't even there. Many men would keep bringing it up and acting like they just saved the world, but not Kevin. He is cool, calm, and collected.

Kevin is well-rounded. He is conversing about

the simplest subject matter and things that matter to him and to the world. I'm elated that he isn't talking about work. Dates often turn into gripe sessions where people bash their employers. Kevin only mentions work once.

"So Sheena, I'm taking an office position here in D.C. It's effective in two weeks. No more traveling all the time. I may travel once in a while, but not weeks and months as it is now," Kevin narrates.

I ask, "How do you feel about that? Is that something you want or is it being forced upon you?"

"Actually it's great! I'm happy with it. I'm tired of the airport layovers and hotel rooms. I'm missing out on many important facets of life because of my career," Kevin says.

"Congratulations! I'm glad for you. I know how tiring traveling can be. I travel for my company sometimes and all the cities and airports have just lost their appeal. If you've seen one, you've seen them all," I say.

"Totally agree. Hopefully, you will allow me to take you out again in the near future. I'll be around now. I would love the company of an intelligent and exquisite woman such as yourself," says Kevin.

"That sounds like a plan to me. We can definitely do this again," I say.

"Cool, I'll hold you to it," Kevin states.

Kevin tells the waiter to bring the check. I

offer to pay the tip, but Kevin will not have it. He wants to pay for the entire meal because he's obviously a gentleman and it is our first meeting. In my book, any man who is a real man will pay for the first date. Hell, he is the one who extended the offer.

After he pays, he walks me to the valet. I give the ticket to the valet attendant to get my car. As I hand him my valet ticket, Kevin is handing a ticket to the other valet attendant along with a nice tip. This man has class. Hopefully, I'll get a chance to see what his car looks like. I know it's something nice because he seems to have expensive taste. The restaurant, the sunglasses he's wearing, and his seemingly brand new shoes speak volumes for the type of man he is. As luck would have it, my car comes before his does. I guess I'll have to wait to see his car. It isn't a big deal anyway. A car is a car.

I head home thinking about the wonderful evening with Kevin. I'm actually a little exhausted, so I head straight to the shower. As I exit the shower, my phone chimes with a message. Surprisingly, when I check my phone, I have three messages. One from Kevin ensuring I made it home safely, one from Eric making sure everything's okay since I canceled on him, and one from Ilesha trying to get details of the evening. I respond to Kevin and Eric. I'll see Ilesha tomorrow to give her details. I slip on my nightie and crawl into bed.

I am well refreshed after a good night of sleep. I seem to be sleeping better now that I have a prospect in my life, actually two prospects. I'm meeting the girls at noon for lunch. I know they will be questioning me about what happened with Kevin last night. It's customary for us to have a debrief session after one of us has a date or does something out of the ordinary. I'm glad that it's my turn to be in the hot seat. I need the excitement of having a new mate. It's like it keeps my blood flowing and adrenaline pumping.

I get dressed and meet the girls at the eatery precisely at noon. To my surprise, Ilesha is on time. How did she manage to do that? Rachel must have told her an earlier time. Sometimes we have to trick Ilesha into being on time. Rachel is punctual as always.

"Hey girls!" I say.

"What's going on Diva?" asks Rachel.

"Hey girl," Ilesha responds.

"Let's sit by the window. I want to see some of that sun shining in. It's pretty outside today," I say.

Ilesha says, "I bet it is pretty outside for you. You are on a roll!"

"I don't know what you are talking about," I retort.

Of course I know what she's referring to, but I decide to play dumb. I hope how happy I am isn't showing because if something goes wrong with these guys, my devastation will be epic. I will downplay it just a little.

"The hell with all the small talk. What happened last night?" Ilesha asks. "I assume things went well since I didn't get a text back."

Rachel chants, "Details! Details!"

"Last night was great! The conversation was very refreshing. The food was fantastic and he was more than a gentleman. On top of that, he dropped some heavy news on me," I narrate.

"He's gay and doesn't like women. I knew it! That man is too handsome and well-groomed to not be gay," states Ilesha.

"No girl! You are silly. He is heterosexual; I can assure you that," I respond.

"Oh my gosh! You gave up the goods to him?" asks Rachel.

"Nooooo I didn't, but I can tell from his treatment of me that he's interested in women. He wants me," I tell them.

"Well, what big news did he drop on you?" asks Ilesha.

"He said he's going to take a new job in town and will no longer be traveling weeks or months at a time. He will be stationary for the most part. He wants to spend time with me and get to know me better," I say.

Rachel asks, "That's great! But what about Eric?"

"Good question Rachel! Put her in the hot seat!" says Ilesha.

"I know. I thought about him too. I will

continue the same relationship I currently have with Eric. We are not exclusive and are just hanging. Kevin and I will also have the same friendly relationship," I explain.

"Well as long as you are keeping it friendly, it's nothing wrong with it," comments Rachel.

"Look at it like a backup plan. You get to know both of them at the same time. Eventually, one of them will do something stupid and then you can stop chilling with him. Then make the other one your man," says Ilesha.

"Men do it all the time. Sage told me about that when we were hanging out. It's called 'The Substitution'," I say.

"Although he has his ways, Sage definitely puts women on to the games men play," says Ilesha.

"Yes, he does have his ways," says Rachel.

I actually like what Ilesha says. She's normally over the top with her solutions to my problems, but this idea is sensible and simple. I don't have a problem with having options. What's the harm in hanging with both of them if I'm not committed to either one of them? I will wait for one of them to screw up and then I can get serious with the other. It's basically an insurance plan. I have to cover my back.

CHAPTER 7

It is now October and the weather is beginning to change. The temperature is starting to dip and people are hanging outside less and less. I have put my summer clothes away and have unveiled my fall and winter gear. It has been several months since I decided to date two men with no strings attached. Unlike the season, there is no change for me. I am still dating both men and having a lot of fun doing it. They both take me where I want to go and they aren't pressuring me about having sex with them. Minus sex, I'm having my cake and eating it too. I need to make a decision quickly about which one I will date exclusively. If I don't, I may lose both of them and never be married as I desire so much. My initial plan of waiting for one of them to slip up is not working. They are both impeccable. No chinks in their armor.

Kevin is on his way over now so we can watch a movie or two. It's a chilly night tonight and I don't feel like going outside. Eric wanted to do something tonight, but I told him no because I already had plans to hang with the girls. I hate lying, but I really want to spend time with Kevin. A relaxing evening in the house is all I'm looking for tonight. I hope he picks an interesting movie. It's a surprise for me. Kevin told me to trust that he will pick something entertaining. He's normally pretty good at it. So far, he hasn't chosen a loser.

Kevin arrives at 8 p.m. sharp. He smells great like always. I love the way his Versace cologne mixes with his natural body scent. It drives me crazy inside. Once again, Kevin has picked a movie that I want to see. I'm really in the mood for a comedy and he has one. I can always count on him to get me where I need to be. There are so many slack men out there that it's a great feeling to have one who isn't slack.

We go upstairs to get our movie night started. The movie is hilarious and I can't stop laughing. I also can't help but notice that my phone keeps lighting up. I'm glad I have it sitting out of Kevin's line of sight because he would see it too and possibly become curious. I get up to check the phone when the movie ends and see that Eric has sent me a message and called. Also, the girls are having a group chat which is why my phone keeps lighting up. I respond to a few of the text messages and then Kevin and I chat for a while. I hear Kevin's stomach growl.

"Are you hungry?" I ask.

"Actually, I am. I wasn't hungry when I got here, but you know how that goes," Kevin responds.

"I am too. I'm in the mood for pizza," I respond.

"I'm cool with pizza. Haven't eaten it in forever," says Kevin.

I order the pizza for delivery. There's no need to leave the house if we don't have to. I inform Kevin that the pizza is my treat. He never lets me pay for anything, but this time he doesn't have a choice. Thirty minutes later the doorbell rings.

"Kevin, I'll go get the pizza," I say.

I grab my wallet and head downstairs while Kevin heads to the bathroom to wash his hands.

When I open the door, the pizza man is standing on the porch. Unfortunately, my attention is focused on Eric's car parked in front of my house. I'm thinking, why is his car out here? As I look at his car, he gets out and approaches the porch. I'm sweating bullets now. If Eric and Kevin come across one another I will surely lose both of them. This is bananas! I can't lose them. They are both great guys. A woman may not find one good man in a lifetime and I've been lucky enough to find two. I wonder if they will curse me out or just fight one another. I think Eric will get beat down if they fight. It could get even worse! What if one of them pulls out a gun and shoots the other? It will be all my fault. I would be devastated if that happens. I have to think fast.

"What's up Sheena? Is everything alright?" Eric asks.

"Ain't much. Just ordering some pizza. Everything is fine. Why wouldn't it be?" I ask.

"Great, I was worried when I called and texted you and didn't receive a response. So I'm here to check on you," Eric explains.

I really want to curse him out for stopping by my place unannounced and without my approval. I'm really not a fan of people popping up at my house. On top of that, I already told him we were having a girls' night. I decide against letting him have it because I know that will start a long discussion and I don't have time for it. I need him to leave as quickly as possible. Kevin has to be wondering what's taking so long. If he comes downstairs, he will see Eric and begin asking questions. I will get at Eric about how I feel later. Now just isn't the time.

"Oh okay, I understand. I'm good to go. Let me pay for this pizza and get back to my girl time," I say.

Eric starts walking back to his car. I walk back to the porch to pay for the pizza. The door is slightly cracked and I can see Kevin at the top of the staircase. He is about to start walking down the stairs. Even if he comes all the way down, I will be in the clear because Eric will already be in his car and up the street. Just as I'm breathing easy, Eric calls out to the pizza man. He wants to pay for the pizza. I start sweating bullets again because now Kevin's walking down the stairs. If I open the door and he sees Eric and the pizza man talking, I am going to cry. As Kevin walks down the steps, he calls out to me.

"Sheena, are you good down there? What's taking so long?" he asks.

I have the pizza in my hands and Eric is by the pizza man's car paying for the pie. I should just run into the house and close the door, but Eric and the pizza guy are in the direct line of sight of the door's opening. Kevin would see them for sure.

"Yes baby, I'm good. Just waiting on my change," I reply as I look back through the door's opening.

He is still walking down the steps and is almost at the door. I hope he doesn't have his phone on him. I call his phone hoping that it's still upstairs. I hear it faintly ringing, so I know it's not on him. He turns around and goes back upstairs to grab his phone. After he clears the steps, I wave at Eric and open the door to go back inside and head upstairs. Kevin is completely clueless about what was going on. He simply mentions that I should use the phone lock being that I dialed him up in error. Meanwhile, I'm a bit shaken. My heart is beating like a stampede of cattle. That was an extremely intense moment. I need a drink after almost being caught out there like a person on an episode of Cheaters.

I don't see how men and women are able to cheat and carry on like it's nothing. I'm not committed to Eric or Kevin and yet I'm a nervous wreck. I can't imagine how nervous I would be if one of them was my man and I was cheating. It takes some pretty big balls to pull this sort of thing off and I just don't have them. I have to do something before the empire comes crumbling down.

I decide to go to the kitchen and grab a glass of wine to help me calm down. I don't want Kevin to notice that I'm a bit flustered. I can't get this out of my mind, so hopefully a glass of wine will fit the bill.

"Kevin, do you want a drink?" I yell out.

"No, I'm good on the drink. Pizza and alcohol isn't a good mix for me," Kevin says.

I reply, "I understand."

The drink is starting to calm my nerves. Kevin and I enjoy the rest of the night. The pizza is great and the second movie is good too. Overall, I'm really just enjoying his companionship. He is so real and straight-forward without being mean or harsh. The drink has me a little horny too. I can't even blame the drink, I'm just horny. The sex drought I'm going through needs to come to a close. Tonight is not the night though. It has gotten late.

"Kevin, it's late and I'm ready to go to bed. You can spend the night and sleep in the guest bedroom if you choose," I say.

"I will head home. I have some stuff I need to do in the morning," Kevin replies.

I walk Kevin downstairs. When we get to the door, he gives me a soft and sensual kiss on my neck. I actually love the placement of the kiss and how erotic it is. I give him a good night hug. While we are hugging he caresses my behind almost like he's doing it by accident, but it is still very noticeable. He then gives me a long kiss good night and walks out the door.

I want to call the girls right now and tell them what happened to me tonight, but I would rather tell them in person. This story is better if I have them in front of me. I know Ilesha is going to have something crazy to say, while Rachel will have something more insightful to share.

The next day I hit the girls up to tell them to come over to the house, so I can tell them what happened. They arrive at the house around noon and we talk about last night's happenings.

"Girl, that is crazy. I know if that was me, I never would've made it. I probably would have broken down in the middle of it all and confessed what I was up to," Rachel says.

"Not me. I would've been fine. I would have cursed Eric out for stalking me like that. There is no telling how long he was out there waiting. Maybe hours," says Ilesha.

"You would've blown your cover if you would have done that. It definitely wasn't worth that," I reply.

Ilesha replies, "I know, but it's the principle behind it. Nobody disrespects me and gets away with it."

Rachel states, "It wasn't disrespectful. He was just checking on her. I think it's kinda sweet."

"Believe that shit if you want to. He was snooping and almost found what he was looking for. Men snoop just like women do, but act like it's only us who do it. Damn hypocrites," Ilesha states.

"Sweet or not, I'm definitely going to address the situation today. As soon as you leave, I'm giving him a buzz. Even if Kevin wasn't upstairs, I still don't like for men to just drop by unexpectedly. I think it's rude," I explain.

"I agree, but your situation is more complicated than that. What are you going to do about dating both of them?" asks Rachel.

"That's the million dollar question right there. You have to pick one. You're not built to play this game and you're risking losing both of them," Ilesha says.

"Who do you like more?" asks Rachel.

"That's the hard part. I like both of them equally. They both have great qualities that I love. What one of them doesn't have, the other one does. I could easily be with either one of them," I explain.

"Well you can't have them both, so you have to make a choice. I'm not saying it will be an easy choice, but you have to decide at some point," says Rachel.

I know they are right. I can't risk losing them both, so I have to make a decision soon. Last night was too close of a call. I'll have a head full of grey hairs if that happens again. I don't want grey hairs before I'm thirty or to be without a man.

"What criteria should I use to determine which suitor to choose?" I ask.

"It's simple. Make a checklist of all the things you want out of a man and then mark all the items on the list that apply to Kevin and Eric respectively. Whoever has more of what you want is the right choice," Rachel narrates.

Ilesha states, "I like that idea. You can even assign weights to the items on your list so that the more important items carry more weight than the others."

"Rachel, that is a great idea! I love it. I'm gonna start that today. It shouldn't take too long," I say.

"Thanks, I use that checklist all the time at work. If I have to cut a position that two people have, that's how I get it done. It makes an already difficult task just a little bit easier," Rachel says.

The girls leave and I begin to work on my list. I create a spreadsheet to help me organize all of the things I'm looking for and the characteristics they possess. The list is coming along effortlessly. I'm checking off items that they both have or only one has and assigning different weights to the categories. I eventually hit a major snag. There is no getting around this item. It is a must have. I am not willing to settle on this one and it's heavily weighted. There is no way I can figure this out on my own. Three minds are better than one. I'm calling the girls to see what advice they have to offer.

"Hey girl. I have an emergency, but hold on. I gotta call Ilesha. I need double help on this one," I say.

"K," Rachel says.

"Hey girl. How's your list going?" Ilesha asks as she answers the phone.

I add Rachel to the conference call and we begin to talk.

"I have a major issue with my list. I can't get my mind around this item. I keep trying, but I have no solution to the dilemma," I say.

"Ooh, I think I know what it is. I thought about you earlier when something came to mind. But go ahead," Ilesha says.

"I'm lost. The list is so simple," says Rachel.

"I don't have a problem with making the list. It's the part of the list that I don't have an answer for nor do I have a solution to fix it," I say.

"We heard you say that the first time! What is it?" Ilesha asks emphatically.

"One of the most important items on my list is sex and I have no reference point because I haven't slept with either one of them. I was rolling right along with my list and then I hit this road block," I explain.

"I see how that's a major problem. I hadn't even thought about the sex thing. That is important, especially knowing they are good candidates otherwise," Rachel says.

Ilesha states, "Yeah, that's high on the must have list. A man definitely has to put it down. He has to be able to sex me good vaginally, orally, and anally."

Rachel screams, "Okay, that was TMI! I did not need all of that! Just a freak!"

"Call it what you want, but it has to be done right. Whatever you like. He cannot be off his 'A' game when it comes to sex," Ilesha says.

"Girl, you know you nasty. Always have been and always will be. But my situation is a real conundrum. What should I do?" I inquire.

"Well, I don't think your situation is too difficult to figure out. You know you need to know how they both perform sexually, so you know what you have to do. It's just a matter of which one," Ilesha narrates.

I say, "I knew you would say that."

Rachel replies, "I agree with her. You will unquestionably have to choose one to have a night of passion with. The only way to know how they are sexually is to have sex."

Oh shit, Rachel agrees with Ilesha. I know at this point that this is the way to go. I'm trying to avoid having sex with either one of them for a little longer, but I guess my time has run out.

"So which one should I choose? I'm equally attracted to both of them. Are you two saying that I should sleep with both of them?" I ask.

Ilesha says, "I would. Plus, that's the only way to compare the two. You have to fuck them both."

Rachel says, "Now I disagree with her on that. You only need to know if one of them is good in bed because you just want to be sure your man possesses sexual prowess, therefore pick one to sleep with. Hopefully, it's mind blowing sex filled with multiple orgasms and you can choose him. You do not need to sleep with both."

"I see where you are coming from. Now I just need a little bit of luck in picking the one with great sex," I say.

"Pretty much. Otherwise if you pick wrong, you will still end up sleeping with both of them anyway. That will be two new partners on your list in a very short time span," Ilesha warns.

"Choose well girl. I would hate to be you right now," says Rachel.

I thank them for their advice and then we end the call. I already know that I'm picking Kevin to have sex with first. The way he kissed me and touched me the other night is still at the forefront of my thoughts. I just hope he can deliver the goods with the same satisfaction he gave me with the kiss. He is a very masculine man, so I know when he gives it to me it will be rough and rugged. I'm a big girl and I can take it. There will be a lot of hair pulling and ass spanking, I'm sure. I can't wait for him to get on this. It has been so long since I had some that I may need to stretch. It'll be super embarrassing if I catch a charley horse while I'm trying to get my freak on. I hope all my moves still work like they used to.

I wonder what I'm going to wear. I have plenty of sexy lingerie that I could wear. Although that's the case, I'm going to buy something brand new. I always feel more confident when I have on new clothes, so this is no different. I'm even going to get my hair done and I'm hoping to sweat it out. I want everything to be perfect. Additionally, I'll make an appointment to get a Brazilian Wax and while I'm there, I'll go ahead and get my eye brows waxed. I am going all out. I need to check with Kevin to see which night he's free. Let me call him.

"Hi Kevin!" I say.

"What's up lady? How are you?" he asks.

I reply, "I'm great. Thank you."

I ask Kevin what he's doing this Friday coming up. He informs me that he's not doing much of anything and that he hopes to see me on Friday. I tell him that Friday is a good day for us to chill. We decide to go see a play and grab a bite to eat afterwards. He tells me that he's looking forward to a great evening. I utter his words back to him. I start to tell him to bring a change of clothes, so he can spend the night, but I choose not to. If I tell him that, he may know that sex is forthcoming. I don't want anything to be unnatural about Friday night. Besides, if I decide to change my mind, I don't want him to be upset. Men always think they are going to get sex if a woman invites them over, especially for the night. I hope this week goes by fast because I am ready to unload on Kevin. Chances are this week will drag by because I want Friday to arrive not now, but right now!

CHAPTER 8

Friday is here! The week actually flew past. I have everything all set up for tonight. Once I leave work, I'm going home to get a nap. After I wake up, it'll be time to get ready for the night. I want to be energized for Kevin and give him the best of me, so my nap is totally necessary. Today is super busy at work. The phones have not stopped ringing and none of my appointments have canceled thus far. I'm good either way. There's only an hour left in the workday and then I'm out of here. I haven't been this excited and nervous about sex since prom night.

What if he doesn't like it? That will be a huge letdown. I can't take rejection like that. Even worse, what if I don't like his performance? I would have given him my body only to be rewarded with a poor performance. I hope his package isn't small or doesn't run out of gas before I reach my climax. What if his soldier won't stand up at all? Is that a sign that he's not attracted to me? How embarrassing would that be if I can't even get him aroused?

There is just too much to think about. If he performs oral sex on me, am I obligated to give him head? Should I be the aggressor or should I let him take the lead? My mind is all over the place. I'm over thinking this. I need a more simple approach. Rachel will know what to do. Where's my phone?

"Hey Rachel. What you doing?" I ask.

"Sitting in my office, wrapping things up. Ready to get out of here," Rachel replies.

"You don't know how much I feel you on that. I'm ready to get out of here myself. Listen, I need your advice about tonight," I say.

I ask, "Do you think I should be the aggressor tonight when it comes time to give him the cookie?"

She replies, in her reassuring tone, "No, girl. You want to do what comes natural. You normally let the guy take the lead, so I suggest you do the same. Also, you don't want to seem desperate for him."

"I know, but what if he doesn't shoot for sex? What if he lays back and doesn't make a move?" I ask.

Rachel questions, "Why are you so worried?"

"I have been pretty clear about not being ready for sex," I reply.

"Again, be yourself. Don't go out of your way to give yourself to him. Remember that you are the prize. What you can do is drop subtle hints to let him know that you want to sex him. He is a college educated man, so he should pick up on the clues. If not, it must not be meant to be tonight," Rachel replies.

"Alright, girl. Thanks for letting me bother you," I say.

Rachel says, "Stop it. You know my shoulder is yours anytime you need to lean on it."

I get off the phone with Rachel and pack up my stuff at work. It is finally time to go. I had such a busy day that a drink or two and a good night out is just what the doctor ordered. I drive home and immediately peel off my clothes. I jump right into bed and grab a quick power nap.

An hour later, I awake from my nap and take a shower. After the shower, I apply my makeup and begin getting dressed. I'm having Kevin pick me up from here, so he has to bring me back home. That'll make it less obvious that I'm trying to give him some. My leopard print bra and panty set is perfect for the night. I have to be prepared just in case I don't have a chance to slip into my lingerie. At least, I'll still be sexy with my matching bra and panty set. I may look disheveled and uncoordinated if my undergarments don't match.

Kevin is right on time. He is very punctual. I wonder if he has always been this way or if he's just putting on a front to win me over in an effort to ultimately get some. He gets out of the car and rings the doorbell. As I open the door, he greets me and presents me with a gift. I'm not expecting a gift, so the extra effort to put a smile on my face is certainly appreciated. It's small things like this, which make me adore him so much. It's not often you find a handsome man who's not conceited and is sincere. I'm not opening the gift now because we have to leave to be on time for the show. As always, he is very well dressed and groomed. He doesn't have one hair out of place. Without contest, Kevin looks like the type of guy I should be paired with. I think we make a beautiful couple.

We are going to watch a play at Constitution Hall. That place brings back many years of memories from undergrad. That's where me and the girls used to attend the step shows from homecoming week at the real HU. We even performed in the step show one year after we became sorority members. I hope we have good seats. I don't like sitting too far from the stage because I can barely see what's going on. I enjoy shows more when I can clearly see the actors and actresses.

We pull up to the theatre and park the car. Kevin is so virile, yet so smooth. He opens the car door for me and gives me his hand to hold as I stand up. He is really laying it on thick. We walk into the hall and an attendant shows us to our seats. I should have known that Kevin would have secured great seats. He's just that type of guy. Nose bleed seats aren't his style, so naturally we have floor seats. I wonder how he was able to secure floor seats on such short notice. He isn't even acting like it's a big deal. It's such a turn on to me the way he makes things happen and makes it appear effortless.

The show is great. It's a romantic comedy and we can't stop laughing. The romance part of the play is okay, but I'm really only worried about the romance that's going to happen at my place tonight. The play takes an intermission, so we walk to the concession stand. As we stand in line waiting to order, I see a glimpse of someone resembling Eric. I know he didn't end up coming to the same play as I did. My luck is the worst. Of all places to end up in D.C., did we really have to come to the same place?

I should have known he would be here though. He's an avid fan of the performing arts. If he sees me, will he approach me? What would he say? I can't worry about that right now. Honestly, Eric can't be mad because I'm not his lady. He is kind of in touch with his feelings though, so he probably would be upset. Oh well, you only live once. I'll just enjoy my night and hope for the best.

"You good?" Kevin asks.

He must sense that my nerves are a little messed up from seeing Eric. I need to play things off better, but it's just not in my nature. My friends always tell me I need to work on my poker face.

"Yes, I'm fine. Why do you ask?" I question.

Kevin replies, "I just want to make sure you're enjoying everything. The play and my company."

I am so glad he didn't sense anything. I feel like I have a sign on my face that reads *Eric is here and Sheena is guilty*.

"Yes, Kevin. The night is perfect so far. You and the play," I reply.

"Alright cool. That's my goal. If you are good, then I am too," he states.

Standing on the long concession line has taken up most of the intermission time. We have just enough time to grab our snack and get back to our seats. The rest of the play is funny and the ending is unpredictable. After the play, we walk through the lobby to exit when we get stopped by all of the congestion in the hallway. While we're stationary, I feel someone tapping me on my shoulder.

I know it's Eric. How did he end up behind me? He wasn't sitting anywhere near us. I looked several times. Maybe he saw me during the show. We did have floor seats and could be seen from many different vantage points. I know I have aged ten years in the three seconds that have passed. I'm reluctant to turn around because I don't want to see the disappointment in Eric's face or have to explain to Kevin what's going on. Tonight is too perfect.

I slowly turn around and to my surprise I see Rachel. She's at the show too. I've never been happier to see her in my life. She received some tickets last minute and came to the show with her boyfriend. We talk to them until the congestion dissipates.

Kevin asks, "How did you like the rest of the play?"

"I loved the ending of the play. It was the opposite of what I expected to happen. I can normally predict what's going to happen half way through the plot. I was way off this time," I explain.

The play was unpredictable like how my life is right now. It's rather exciting not knowing what's going to happen, but it's also nerve wrecking.

"Even Michael Jordan missed a shot or two in a game. We are all wrong sometimes. Some people are just wrong more often than others. I thought it was pretty good too," says Kevin.

We go eat dinner at a diner that Kevin suggests. The service is flawless. I anticipated the service to be pretty bad because the diners I've been to are normally that way. However, the food comes out quickly and we are on our way back to my house before I know it.

We drive to my house and pull up in front. Now is the moment of truth. What will Kevin do? Is he going to make a move or not? I guess I will throw him a hint like Rachel said I should.

Kevin comes around to the passenger side to open my door. I get out of the vehicle and we walk to the house.

As I open the door, I say, "Kevin thanks for a wonderful night. I really enjoyed everything. It was fun."

Kevin replies, "The pleasure was all mine. Chilling with a gorgeous and intelligent woman is always a good look."

Kevin leans in and gives me a kiss that is heavenly. I feel myself getting wet as he grabs me close.

"If you don't have anything to do in the morning, you should come inside. At least come in so I can open the gift you gave me. I've been excited about the gift all evening," I say.

"Sure, I'll come in. I'm free for the early part of tomorrow," Kevin replies.

We walk into the house and I immediately reach for the gift. I eagerly open the box like a child opening a gift on Christmas Day. The box contains a silver chain with a charm that I don't recognize. The charm is a simply designed leaf that doesn't intrigue my tastes. I don't tell Kevin, but I'm a bit disappointed in the gift. I'm not ungrateful, but the chain and charm don't impress me the way Kevin has been impressing me all night. Am I wrong for not liking the gift? I fake as if I like the gift. I don't want to hurt his feelings.

I say, "I love it. Thank you so much."

Kevin replies, "I'm glad you love it. I was hoping you would."

"I love silver, but I don't recognize the leaf," I reply.

"I know silver is your thing, but let me explain the meaning behind the charm and necklace. The leaf is from the Fig Tree. The Fig Tree has been a symbol of unity for centuries. It also has the deepest running roots of all trees, running four hundred feet deep. The way the chain is braided is symbolic of the roots of the tree. I hope we can be a unit and our relationship runs just as deep as the tree's roots," he narrates.

After he explains the gift, I am speechless. The thoughtfulness of the gift is like nothing I've ever received. Most men try to excite women with expensive gifts, while paying no attention to detail or sentiment. I'm extremely moved by his gesture and thoughtful words. I can't help but to shed a few tears.

Kevin holds me against his firm chest and rubs my back. Then he puts the necklace around my neck. I lead Kevin upstairs to my room. When we get to my room, Kevin begins kissing on me again. He slightly raises my head as he kisses me down my neck and collar bone. I stop him momentarily.

"Let me freshen up. We'll finish what you've started soon. There's fresh linen in the bathroom downstairs if you want to freshen up as well. There's soap in there too," I say.

"Oh, okay. Is there soap too?" Kevin asks sarcastically.

I chuckle in response to his sarcasm. I guess my comment was a little ridiculous. I jump in the shower in an attempt to get ready for my tryst. I vaguely hear the chime from my alarm system letting me know the front door is open. I think Kevin must have had to run to the car for something. I love the way this shower gel smells. I hope Kevin likes it more than I do. I have my new lingerie set hanging in the bathroom waiting for me to jump into it. I am so ready. I hope he's almost done freshening up because I don't want to wait.

I hear my bathroom door open and before I know it, Kevin is in the shower with me. His hard, muscular, naked body is pressed up against mine. This man's body is perfect. I can't imagine he has more than 5% body fat. As he kisses me behind my ear and around my neck, his firm chest is rhythmically rubbing up against my nipples. This is not what I envisioned for the night, but it works. This is a pleasant surprise!

Kevin turns me around and washes my back while he massages it. I feel his erect penis pressed up against my tight ass while he caresses my back. He grabs me around my waist and begins to kiss me down my back. Water is splashing everywhere and the bathroom is steamy like fog creeping around a cemetery in a scary movie.

I'm not sure if the bathroom is foggy from us or from the steam of the water. Either way, the fog is making me even more aroused. Kevin turns me around and looks me in my eyes. His eyes are mesmerizing and filled with passion.

Kevin says, "It's moments like this that make me glad I no longer travel for work. It's a good woman like you who makes me want to fall asleep and wake up next to you every day."

His solid roll of quarters is poking me in my stomach and I want to climb his body and ride his dick until it's limp. He kisses my lips while he delicately gropes my breasts. I close my eyes and feel his smooth juicy lips licking my nipples and areola. Between all of this foreplay and the length of time since I've had an orgasm, I might cum from him licking my nipples. He slides one hand around my back and grabs my left booty cheek and with his free hand he fondles my clit.

I feel my knees about to buckle from the sensation. The feeling is so intense that it feels like one long orgasm only I'm not cumming. I love the way my body responds to his touch. After he rubs my clit, he licks me down my stomach and nuzzles my clitoris. His tongue on my pussy feels like air to someone who is suffocating. If he keeps this up, I am going to burst all over his face. He thinks his face is wet now from the shower water, wait until I release. He might honestly drown if I erupt.

Kevin stands up straight and says, "We'll finish

the rest of this in a minute."

He continues washing and I get out of the shower. I exit the shower, so I can dry off and oil up. This is great because now I can put on the lingerie set I purchased. I'm excited that he'll get to see me in it. I bought it especially for this night.

Kevin finishes washing and drying about the same time I finish putting on my edible oil and slipping on my seductive wear. He grabs me by the hand and opens the bathroom door. As the door opens, I see iris petals placed all over my bedroom. There are vanilla scented candles strategically positioned around the room. The scent is calming and enticing all at once. I've never had a man to put forth so much effort. This man of steel definitely has a romantic and sensitive side.

"You really know how to set a mood. This is amazing!" I say.

I'm wondering if the sex will be as amazing as his foreplay. I hope so because with all of this hype, anything less than a ten will certainly be a disappointment.

He replies, "I'm glad you like it."

I turn on some music to further set the mood. With a scene like this, there is no way that music wouldn't be involved. Kevin has set a mood for slow jams, so I set the playlist to all slow music. Kevin motions me to dance with him. We sway side to side as one. He's naked and I'm in my cheetah print lingerie set.

"Did I tell you that you are beautiful?" Kevin asks.

"No you didn't. But your friend down there is giving it away," I say.

Conversation is over at this point. He lies me down on the bed, looks me in my eyes, and runs his fingers through my hair as he kisses me. I wrap my arms around him while he sucks my bottom lip. Kevin raises my arms above my head and pins them down with one hand as he feathers my body with the other. His mint scented breath is making waves of moisture form in my sweet spot as he nibbles on my ear. He proceeds by pulling my breasts out of my bra and begins licking and kissing them. He takes his time with each one. No neglect here. He makes me feel as if I'm a pot of gold and he intends to cherish every coin from top to bottom. This is pleasure at its finest. His hand makes it down to my vagina and he slides my panties over so he has access to my pussy.

He's rubbing and caressing the outside of my vagina. *Please put your dick in.* I am ready to explode. My hormones are raging like a bull. Kevin lifts up my hood and begins to subtly smooch my soaked vaginal area. He pulls my thong clean off my body and buries his face into my womb. He uses his tongue to penetrate my walls. In and out and then he licks my clit and repeats the motion. I feel my body tingling and getting hotter, so I know I am about to explode. I grab his head and pull it closer into my pussy. I'm swerving and grinding and moving his head to maximize the sensation. I know he probably can't breathe, but I'm almost there.

I scream, "Right there! Don't move!"

His tongue is alternating between slow calculated strokes and faster stimulating strokes all around my clit. He has a nice motion going on. It's like his tongue was made to lick me down there. My body starts to go into deep convulsions as I release the months of pent up stress, frustration, and horniness all over his face. After the big shakes, there are several tremors to follow. He handles them like a champ because he keeps on eating and doesn't flinch one bit. My body goes limp after I release. My energy flushes out of every fiber of my being.

Kevin quickly wipes his face and immediately jumps into my soaking wet ocean and strokes through it with his vessel. His pumps are slow and methodical. He slowly grinds my body to the beat of the music. He runs his fingers through my hair as he softly kisses my body. His pole is long, golden, and hard. He treats my body like a prized possession. The more he strokes me, the more my energy comes back. His penis rests in my pocket like a tailored fitted suit fits a man's body.

Kevin stops penetrating me from between my legs and flips me onto my stomach. He puts a pillow under my stomach which makes my booty stick up higher into the air. He begins rubbing my clit, while eating me from behind. I am wet like a super saturated sponge. I can't get any wetter. Just when I think I've reached my maximum euphoria, he slides his staff back into me. I reach a new level of ecstasy as I feel his pole extend into my stomach. I never knew I could feel a dick in my stomach.

He's gripping my ass with his large strong hands. He thrusts me from behind and I can feel my derriere jiggle with every pump.

"Kevin!" I scream.

"Yes baby," Kevin says in his low seductive voice.

His voice is low and mellow. He strokes me from behind as he reaches under me and plays with my nipples. Every touch he makes sends me into a different zone. As he thrusts me, I push my booty back onto his rod. His penetration goes deeper and deeper every time I push back. All I can do is bite the sheets to keep from pulling my hair out. Kevin switches his angle of penetration. He places me on my side and he lies on his side as well. Now his dick is slowly massaging my vaginal wall as he goes in and out. All I hear is the sound of my gushing wet coochie. I feel my body heating up again. With every stroke of his dick, he is rubbing my G-spot. I know it's only a matter of time before I cum again.

I feel Kevin's dick get even harder. He is moaning and grinding even faster now. I'm extremely turned on from hearing him make these sounds. He's about to explode his cream inside of me. I'm cumming all over his dick. While I'm releasing, he begins to release inside of me too. Kevin and I both cum at the same time. He collapses on me and I feel his heart beating through his chest. I feel connected to Kevin. No man has ever made me feel the way I feel now.

"That was incredible," I say.

"I second that notion. You are amazing from head to toe," says Kevin as he places a soft sensual kiss on my stomach.

My body is tingling all over from what Kevin just did to me. I can't even get up. Kevin and I both fall asleep right where we are.

CHAPTER 9

We wake up about ten o'clock the next morning. I am exhausted. Last night was nothing short of amazing. Kevin wants to go to breakfast, but I tell him I'm not going. The girls and I have a date with the gym at noon. I'm also in a rush to tell them about my miraculous night. A little piece of me wants to gloat. I'm so relieved that Kevin performed like a sexual superstar. My search is finally over. I can settle down and see where this leads. No more club hopping for me and no more dating two men. Now I can focus on my relationship with Kevin and make it effloresce.

I meet Rachel and Ilesha at Silver's Gym on schedule. I really don't feel like exercising because I had such a great workout last night. I burned all of the calories I need to burn. I'm going light on the workout today.

As soon as I walk up, I hear, "You better have some juicy details for us today! You better not have gotten scared," says Ilesha.

"Girl stop. If she didn't sleep with Kevin, that's her prerogative," Rachel replies.

"Well, how was your night girl?" Ilesha asks. "Did you fuck him?"

"It was the best night ever! I am thoroughly satisfied with his performance," I say.

"So are you saying that you gave it up?" inquires Ilesha.

"Did I? Oh yeah, I gave it to him last night. Well, maybe I should say he gave it to me," I reply with a huge smile on my face.

"Sounds like Kevin put it down," comments Rachel.

I reply, "He put it down, lifted it back up, and put it down again. The night was simply amazing! He met all of my needs."

"Was he holding or what?" asks Ilesha.

"I'll just say that when he put it in me, it seemed like it was never going to stop. His package is long and satisfying. I could feel him in my ribs the entire time we were sexing. I was overwhelmed with pleasure!" I reply.

"Damn girl, I've felt like a man was in my stomach before, but not the ribs," Ilesha says.

"Now the ribs are a new one for me too. I know that had to hurt," replies Rachel.

I say, "I thought the same thing, but it actually didn't hurt one bit. Kevin's sexual performance was the exact opposite of what I expected. Kevin's day to day personality is real manly and strong. I expected him to be rough and real aggressive during sex. Instead, he was very gentle and soft while we were intimate. He licked and kissed me all over. He even set the mood exquisitely by dropping flowers and lighting candles."

"Ooh, that sounds like my kind of night. Sensual is my style!" says Rachel.

"Licking and kissing! Sounds like somebody got tasted last night!" Ilesha bellows.

"I sure did! He tasted, ate, and devoured my sweet spot. He even made me erupt all over his face. I locked onto his face when I started convulsing and gave him months of pent up stress and frustration," I explain.

Rachel and Ilesha start laughing and cheering me on. They've both experienced locking in on a guy's face and letting him have the full release of juices that he's caused.

Rachel asks, "Was he mad at you for cumming all over him like that?"

"No, not at all. He was all in. When I locked his face in, he seemed to be more turned on and ate even faster. My body went limp after that," I say.

"The only natural response after that is to put his hard dick in your mouth and repay him for treating you," says Ilesha.

"If he gives you oral, it's only fair that you give

it back," says Rachel.

"I would have given him some head with no problem, but before I knew it, he was inside of me stroking like he was a swimmer in an Olympic competition trying to win gold. He even made me cum again from his penetration," I narrate.

"That's awesome! I am shocked that he made you orgasm from eating you out. That's a first for you right?" asks Rachel.

I say, "Yes, that's a first. A couple of guys have gotten close to making me release by performing oral, but none have ever reached the finish line. Pure pleasure!"

"I am so happy for you! He's a great guy and he fucked you good. Get it girl!" says Ilesha.

"I'm happy for you too Sheena. Now we can all triple date together. We can be like those couples from the movies who go on couple's retreats," remarks Rachel.

"Thanks girls, I'm happy. I'm not so happy about ending things with Eric though. He is such a sweetheart. He's considerate and always makes me happy. He and Kevin should just fuse together into one person and then I wouldn't have to drop Eric," I say.

"By the way, there is one thing about the night that I didn't mention. Please don't judge," I say.

"What happened?" asks Rachel.

"Well, we didn't use protection and he came in me," I report, while partially covering my face.

"Girl, that's nothing. I thought you were

going to say something big happened," replies Ilesha.

Rachel says, "You are so naughty! I wouldn't worry though. We have all done that before."

I know I should have used protection, but I got so caught up in the moment that a condom didn't even cross my mind. I don't even know if he had any with him. I think a part of me didn't want to use a rubber anyway. Those things often dry me out and I didn't want Kevin to think that I'm always dry and wasn't aroused. That would've marred my night and I didn't want that.

"That's true. Thanks for making me feel better. I'm meeting with Eric later to tell him that we're just going to be friends," I say.

"You don't need to meet up with him! Send him a text or call him. It's easier and quicker," says Ilesha.

"No, I owe it to him to do this face to face. He has only been kind to me. I respect him more than that. He's going to stop by and we'll chat," I explain.

"I am all for the face to face conversation, but him coming to your place is a bad idea. Meet him at a public place. You never how someone will take a breakup," Rachel says.

"He's cool. It'll be a quick light-hearted conversation. I really don't see him acting up. I'll tell him that you guys are coming over soon after he gets there. In fact, let me get out of here. I'm going to straighten up the house before he gets there. I'll text y'all later," I say.

"Bye girl," says Rachel.

Ilesha teases, "Later hoe!"

When I arrive home, I begin cleaning up all of the flower petals that Kevin placed all over the floor. I want to leave them where they are, but Eric doesn't need to see them. If he sees the flower petals, he will know for sure what I did last night. I don't want him to know my wanting to stop hanging is centered on another man. There's an outline of the huge wet spot on my sheets from where I released all over Kevin's face. I damn near drowned him. I don't have time to change the sheets because Eric will be here in a minute. He isn't coming further than the living room anyway, so it can wait until later.

Eric rings the doorbell just as I finish taking a shower. He must have just left the barber shop because his hairline is extra sharp.

"Smelling and looking good," I say.

"Thanks, you smell great too! You smell like you just got out of the shower," Eric replies.

"Yeah, I did. Me and the girls were at the gym. I didn't want you to catch me all sweaty," I reply.

Eric retorts, "There's nothing wrong with a little bit of sweat. Depending on the circumstances, sweat is all good with me."

I know he's referring to sex, but I don't even comment on it. He always did have a way with words. I start talking to Eric about the status of our relationship, but he cuts me off.

"I want to apologize to you for popping up on you the other night. I didn't mean to interrupt the time with your girls," Eric says.

I say, "I didn't exactly appreciate that, so thanks for the apology. That's not why I asked you over. I want to discuss the future of our relationship."

"Cool, I want to too. What are your thoughts?" Eric asks.

"I think we should just be friends. You are very sweet and considerate, but we should just be cool," I say.

"To be honest with you, that's not what I want. I'm in love with you Sheena and I want to foster our relationship. I think we have an opportunity to share something special. You just said I'm sweet and considerate. You know the man I am," Eric narrates.

I'm at a loss for words. I don't know how to respond to him telling me that he's in love with me. My heart has just filled with an indescribable joy.

"Wait, you love me?" I ask.

Eric moves in close to me and looks me in the eyes and says, "I have loved you for months now. I knew you were special from the first time I met you in the bowling alley. Every day I awake, I think of ways to make you happy. When I sleep, I dream of ways to bring pleasure to your doorstep."

I'm melted ice cream by the time he finishes pouring his heart out. His words are touching my soul. He basically lives to make me happy. Can I turn my back on someone who is that committed to making me happy? I don't know.

Eric continues, "Air is what has allowed me to live life before meeting you. Now, air is Sheena. Food used to nourish me, but now food is Sheena."

His sincerity makes me very emotional and a tear trickles down my cheek. Eric wipes the tear from my cheek and plants a tender kiss on my forehead.

"Me wiping your tear away is symbolic of what I want to be in your life. I want to wipe all of your sorrows away and only afford you tears of joy," Eric says.

He raises my head to be level with his and gives me a hard kiss on my lips. I kiss him back and before I know it, we are engulfed in a full-fledged make out session. I'm tugging on his belt to get his dick out of his pants, while he's ripping my sweat suit off of me. I pull his meat out of his pants, yank his underwear down around his ankles and put his rock solid dick in my mouth. I jerk it in a circular motion and suck it at the same time. Eric is grabbing the back of my head as he pumps my mouth. I am gagging on his erect scepter. He's standing over me with his rod in my mouth like a king over his subjects.

Eric forcefully picks me up in the air and

inserts himself into my pussy. He is holding me in the air as he infiltrates my fortress over and over again. He is gripping my ass cheeks and nibbling on my neck, while I ride his horse. Eric is talking very dirty to me while he thrusts me airborne.

"This is some good pussy! I love it!" Eric screams.

I get right into character with him and start saying dirty things back.

"Make me cream all over you! Hell yeah, fuck me. Fuck this pussy. It's yours!" I scream.

Eric and I are no holds barred in the living room. We have knocked over one of my vases, but it doesn't even matter. We are locked into one another right now and the only thing that will release us is an orgasm. I feel like a jockey in a horse race because that's how hard I'm riding and he's slapping my ass with force.

Eric puts me down and bends me over on the edge of the couch. His heavy thick dick spreads my womb open as he pounds me profusely. I love every minute of it. He is sexing me like this is makeup sex, only we haven't been arguing. This is the perfect definition of pleasure and pain. While he strokes me from behind, I feel him playing with my butthole and it surprisingly feels great. He's rubbing my asshole with his thumb and it adds a new level of excitement to everything he's doing to me. I hope he sticks his finger in my ass.

I think he heard my thoughts. Eric sticks his thumb in my butt and continues to prod me with his pole. The combination of his thick dick, balls slapping my clit, and thumb in my ass makes me lose all my inhibitions.

"Harder damn it! Go deeper! Yes, baby! You know what I like! Give it to me!" I yell.

He stops sexing me for a second to flip me onto my back. I put his staff directly in my mouth and suck it without using my hands. Men, for some reason, are amazed when women suck them off without using their hands. Eric's eyes are rolling back in his head. I know he's enjoying this as much as I am. I am so wrapped up in moment that I want him to burst in my mouth. Instead, Eric carries me upstairs to my bedroom and throws me down on the bed. I am on my back as he re-enters my super soaked pocket of pleasure. He has a direct shot into my tunnel. I feel all of his meat as his dick fondles my G-spot with every reentry. It feels so euphoric that I'm getting close to having an orgasm. I feel my body tingling and the pressure is building up. I am primed for a great release.

The only problem is that I have to urinate. This is the worst possible time to have to use the bathroom. Eric is focused and I'm going to have to stop him, so I don't pee on him. That would be super embarrassing. I don't want to kill my orgasm either. I have to stick with this.

Eric is all over my G-Spot. The sensation is

incredible!

"You like this dick? Huh, you like it?" he asks.

"Yeah, you are getting it so good that you're gonna make me go on myself!" I scream.

Eric screams, "Push it out. Let that pressure out!"

I'm afraid to push it out because I don't want to pee on him or myself, but I begin pushing it out like he demands. Oh my gosh! I feel the greatest release that I've ever felt in my life. I'm ejaculating all over Eric. I'm squirting and the feeling is intense like a bomb exploding. I feel the cum shooting out of me like Spiderman's web.

Eric starts speeding up even more with his thrusts. Each time he pounds my pussy is like a punch from Mike Tyson. He is ready to blow like I just did.

"Ahhhh shit! Yeah, Sheena. Grrr. Whooooo!" Eric screams as he busts a nut.

I say, "It sounds like you needed that. That was extremely intense."

"Yes, baby. I needed that. Seems like I'm not the only one who needed to release. You squirted all over me," comments Eric.

"I know right. I thought I was about to wet myself, but when you said to push it out, I went with what you said," I explain.

"I bet you're glad you listened to me," says Eric.

"Extremely elated. I've never ejaculated

before. I mean, I've had orgasms before, but never squirted. That felt much better and it lasted longer," I narrate.

"I'm shocked. All women can ejaculate, so I figured you would have before. Well, I'm glad I'm your first and only. I guess that's my claim to fame. Pushing it out is what makes you squirt," Eric explains.

I tell Eric to forget about what I said earlier about us parting ways and just being friends. He's happy with my decision to keep seeing him. I give him a wash cloth and soap, so he can cleanup. I need another shower and some counseling from my girls as soon as possible. I am so far past where I want to be. Eric wants to stay after he cleans up, but I tell him he has to leave. I need some alone time to clear my head. After Eric leaves, I change my sheets and get in the shower. It has been a long day and I'm drained. I will call the girls tomorrow to see when I can meet up with them. It's time for bed.

The sun is beaming in my eyes. There is no way it's morning already. I look over at the clock and it's after 11. I never sleep in this late. I feel like I just went to sleep. My body is just so tired. I have had sex with two different men two days straight. My body can't take this, nor can my mind. Let me text the girls and see if they're available for dinner.

Great! They are both free tonight. I'll treat them, since they've been helping me so much.

We are eating at a seafood restaurant tonight. I could use some fish. It's supposed to be brain food and I need all the brain power I can muster. I'm not doing much today. I am just chilling until dinner time.

The day of doing nothing goes by pretty fast. It's already time to meet Ilesha and Rachel for dinner. I drive to the restaurant and walk inside. Rachel is already here like clockwork. Ilesha shows up a few minutes after six. That's basically on time for her because she's normally later than this. I immediately order a drink to help loosen me up.

"Damn, you aren't wasting any time at all! She must have a story to tell," says Ilesha.

Rachel asks, "Is everything okay? What happened?"

"No, I fucked this one up! I totally lost control of the situation," I say.

"How so?" inquires Rachel.

"Don't criticize me, but I slept with Eric last night," I reply in almost a whisper.

"Get the hell outta here! That's one of my numbers. I didn't see this coming!" screams Ilesha.

Rachel says, "This is not what I anticipated, but you'll get through it. No, we'll get through it together. You aren't the first woman to sleep with two men in a short time frame. These things happen."

"Sheena, really? I've done it several times. It's

no big deal," Ilesha says.

"I didn't want this. I told him we should stop hanging out and before I knew it, his dick was in my mouth," I report.

"You gave him head?" Ilesha asks excitedly.

"Sounds like a wild night," Rachel says.

"It was very wild! He picked me up in the air and fucked me, then threw me on the couch and roughed me up. Every minute of it was great. To top it off, he made me squirt all over him when I climaxed," I explain.

"I've never been made to squirt before. I'm jealous," says Rachel.

"You are in sexual heaven. You've gotten some dick two days in a row and both encounters were excellent. Hell, I'm jealous too," says Ilesha.

"Who's better?" asks Rachel.

"They are both great. I can't say one is better than the other. Kevin's package is longer, but Eric's is thicker. Kevin is more sensitive during sex, while Eric is aggressive. Both score a ten from me sexually. That's why I'm so confused. I thought I had it figured out, but now I'm more clueless than I was before," I respond.

"I know you are twisted right now. I would be too. Crazy! I'm sorry you have to go through this," says Ilesha.

"I should have listened to Rachel and not let him come over. I wouldn't be in this situation had I listened to you," I say.

"Well girl, we are past that. We have to deal

with where we are now," says Rachel.

"She's right. Sex with two different men on back to back days can happen. Did he at least wear a condom?" asks Ilesha.

"He did," I answer.

"Who do you care about more? Who do you see yourself with long term?" asks Rachel.

"I have strong feelings for both of them. I can honestly see myself with either of them long term. I'm in love with both of them and sexually they both are amazing. Kevin and Eric are both intelligent and goal oriented. They also share the same family goals as me. I'm stuck," I explain.

"This is quite a situation you have on your hands. You are just going to have to ride this out a little longer. Since you can't choose, it seems like all you can do is let time pass and see where you end up," says Rachel.

"I agree. Unfortunately, you are right back where you started. Something will happen to make your decision easier. Do like men do and date both. You don't have to sex them day after day. You are in control. Give each of them some at your discretion. That's my advice," says Ilesha.

"Girl, it's your show. Take control. Men do it all the time and it's no big deal. Think about how Sage was running game. Nobody was mad at him. It's your time girl. Do your thing," Rachel says.

"I will. I guess my situation isn't all bad. I have two great men! It could be a million times worse. I guess I'm about to be a player," I say.

We continue to converse over dinner and wrap things up. I feel a whole lot better about things. What would I do without my girls – my sisters? I can consistently count on them to calm me down and bring my focus back.

CHAPTER 10

It's a month and a half later and I am knee deep into a tangled web. I'm dating two men and having sexual relations with both of them. Pleasing two men is no easy task. I never saw myself in this situation, but I'm here. I'm in a battle with my scruples everyday about what I'm doing. I'm basically playing both of them and I feel so guilty because I don't know how else I should feel about myself. Am I a hoe? Am I a scandalous female? Are there really other females in the same situation as me? Are my friends talking about me behind my back?

I don't know how much longer I can keep this up. I've been extremely fatigued since I began sleeping with Kevin and Eric. I went from not having sex at all to getting it pretty regularly. I guess my body has to adjust to this new cycle I'm on. Between work and my two new boyfriends, I deserve to be tired. All of this ducking and dodging would break anybody down.

The girls and I are having dinner at a new seafood restaurant that just opened a week ago. It has gotten rave reviews from all of the food critics. I've been craving seafood lately, so we came out to get our eat on.

"This menu has everything on it," says Rachel.

"It sure does and I want everything on it! I am so greedy," I reply.

"Girl, you have been eating everything in sight lately. Is everything cool?" asks Ilesha.

I reply, "Everything's fine. I'm just under a ton of stress between work and these two men. Eating is my way of coping. I'll get it under control. Thanks for asking."

"Eating is not the best remedy for your situation. You need to get back in the gym with us. You are looking a little unlike yourself," Rachel narrates.

"I know. I know. I'm just tired and in a funk," I say.

I order a sample of several different appetizers. I don't know exactly what I want, so I figure I should just order a little of everything. We are enjoying our food and our conversation. The girls ride me about the little weight I've gained, but it's cool. I can burn these few pounds off in no time. A few hours in the gym and I'll be right back in business. It's just difficult finding time between work and servicing my men. My phone is ringing, so I answer it and get up to walk to the restroom.

"You don't have to leave the table to answer the phone. Get your tail back over here!" Ilesha yells.

"Yeah, we won't interrupt your conversation," says Rachel.

"I know you won't bother me, but I have to use the restroom. All in my business," I respond.

Ilesha and Rachel are talking about something as I walk to the restroom. I'm talking to Kevin. He wants to come over tonight after I finish up with dinner. I inform him that I expect it to be a late night, so we can't hang out. The girls and I are going to In the Mix tonight. I don't mind going, since I'm over Sage and his nonsense. I have my own thing going on now, so Sage is irrelevant. I use the restroom and walk back to the table.

"You two were talking about me, weren't you?" I ask.

"You bet your bottom dollar we were!" says Ilesha.

"What were you saying?" I question.

"Well, we are concerned about you. We think your situation is deeper than just being tired and stressed," says Rachel.

"Girl, we think you might be pregnant," Ilesha says bluntly.

"I can't be. I haven't been sick at all," I say.

"You may just be one of the ones who doesn't

get sick or it could be too early for morning sickness. Let's look at your symptoms. You have been abnormally tired, gaining weight, and you can't stop using the bathroom," says Rachel.

"And you've been craving everything in sight," Ilesha chimes in.

"All we are saying is that it's worth it to take a home pregnancy test to at least certify or nullify our suspicions. We can hit the 24 hour pharmacy as soon as we leave here," says Rachel.

"Okay, I'll take one, but I'm not paying for it. It's going to be a waste of time and money," I reply.

"That's fine. I'll pay for it. We can go back to your house and you will take it," says Ilesha.

Rachel summons the waiter over to bring us the check. We immediately go to the pharmacy and pick up a pregnancy test. I'm against it, but I know they won't be satisfied until I prove them wrong.

"Don't get the cheap one," says Rachel.

"Trust me girl. I've taken enough of these to know better than to pick up the cheap test. I know what I'm doing," says Ilesha.

"Can we hurry this up? Does this have to be such a production?" I ask.

"Here it is. We are ready to roll," says Ilesha.

We drive to my house and go upstairs to the bathroom. I take the test, but I'm too nervous to look at it.

"One of you will need to look at this thing

when it's ready and tell me what it says," I say.

We leave the test in the bathroom and go downstairs to chill for a while. We are all silent and wondering what the test says. I am too tired to walk back upstairs and check it myself, but it's killing me not to know. Just as I'm about to tell Ilesha to go get the test, she runs upstairs and grabs it on her own. She runs downstairs with the test and shows Rachel what it indicates. I am the one who is or isn't pregnant and I'm the last to know. Isn't this ironic?

"What does it say?" I ask.

"Congratulations sister!" Rachel exclaims.

I don't know if the congratulations is because she's congratulating me on my future motherhood or because she knows I don't want to be pregnant, so she's congratulating me on not being knocked up.

"Give me the test!" I order.

I am in utter disbelief. The test shows that I'm pregnant, but I just can't believe it. This test has to be wrong. Well, I hope the test is wrong. I have to take another one to be certain. Ilesha goes to the store to get another one. I take that test too and the results are the same. I'm going to be a mom!

"Girl, are you okay? How do you feel about this?" asks Rachel.

"I'm good, I think. Just didn't want this to happen right now. This is so sudden and unexpected. My head is spinning right now," I explain.

"I feel you girl. I know it's sudden, but we are here for you. Auntie Rachel - I love the way that sounds," replies Rachel.

"You know we will do whatever you need us to do. You'll have us here to help you during your pregnancy and afterwards. The village will raise this child. Besides, I need a little person to spoil anyway," says Ilesha.

Rachel says, "A child is a blessing, so don't see it as a burden. Another good thing is that now you can be with the child's father. Your decision has just been made for you. I'm sure Kevin will be excited about this news."

"That's right. You said he wants a family, so he should be right on board with this," says Ilesha.

I'm still in a daze and unable to speak.

"You said you only had unprotected sex with Kevin the first time you had sex with him, so he's most likely the father," Rachel deduces.

I start crying as soon as Rachel says that. I'm horrified about what will happen in the future. What have I gotten myself into? Deception is never a good thing. I am so screwed.

"Why are you crying? What's wrong baby?" asks Rachel.

"Spill the beans. There's something you aren't telling us," says Ilesha.

"Well, I wasn't completely honest with you when I told you about the first time Eric and I had sex. All of the details of the night were completely accurate, except when I said Eric used protection. He really didn't. He released inside of me just as Kevin had done the night before," I mutter as I continue to cry into my hands.

"We are your girls. Why did you lie?" asks Rachel.

"I had sex with two men one day after the other and felt bad about it. On top of that, I let both of them sex me unprotected. I was a bit embarrassed and thought you ladies would come down hard on me for behaving in such a reckless manner," I explain.

Ilesha says, "You can always keep it real with us. We never judge you and you never judge us. That's our code. You know that."

"Yeah girl. You know we got your back unconditionally. You never have to lie to or mislead us," says Rachel.

I reply, "I know and I'm sorry for lying to you. My bad. It won't happen again."

"We forgive you this time. We understand why you did what you did," says Ilesha.

Rachel says, "Yeah, we forgive you, but we need to get you to a doctor or clinic for a blood test. We have to be one hundred percent certain."

I agree with what Rachel says. The best bet is to go to the doctor, so he can do a blood test. I call my doctor two days later and schedule an appointment. Good fortune is on my side because my doctor is able to see me at the end of the week. The sooner, the better.

The week drags by slowly, but eventually my appointment day is here. As luck would have it, I'm now experiencing morning sickness and my breasts are extremely tender. Even taking a shower is a challenge as each water drop feels like a little pellet striking my nipples. The appointment is just a formality at this point because I know for sure I'm with child. I'm actually becoming more and more excited about the thought of motherhood. It is a dream of mine to be a mother. I just want it under better circumstances, but we can't always pick and choose our situations. The doctor confirms that I'm pregnant and informs me that I am six weeks along. I call Rachel and Ilesha and tell them the fantastic news. They are elated for me and for themselves. Rachel and Ilesha will both be godparents.

I am flourishing financially and have the right frame of mind to have a child, but I'm facing a major conflict. I don't know who the father of my child is. I never imagined I would ever be in a position to even utter those words. Kevin or Eric could easily be the father. I have no idea what I should do. Should I pick one of the guys and just tell him he's the father? I can't do that because that would be wrong and what if I'm not right with my guess? I can't have a man raise a child who isn't his because I've been deceitful. It's not like I can hide being pregnant from them either and once I start showing, each man will assume the child is his.

I could have a blood test performed while my child is growing inside of me, but the doctor explained that it's extremely risky. Many complications could come from such a high risk maneuver. It could potentially cause me to miscarry my baby, so that's certainly out of the question. There's no way I'm aborting the pregnancy because I don't believe in that. I am prolife all the way. The only option I have is to tell Kevin and Eric that I'm pregnant and that he will be a father. Once the child is born, I'll have a paternity test performed. Then I'll have to break one of their hearts and tell him he's not the father. I don't think I have any other options. What else can I do? I'll tell both of them tomorrow that they are fathers to be.

It's the next day and I have to meet with Kevin and Eric. They know I want to discuss something with them, but not exactly what. I'm driving to Kevin's house now to meet with him. When I arrive, Kevin greets me pleasantly as he always does.

"What's up beautiful? How are you?" he asks.

I really don't feel like small talk, so I indulge in the minor conversation briefly and get right to my real reason for coming over.

"I have some very important information to share with you. I came to tell you as soon as I found out. It's a very serious matter," I say.

"I appreciate that. Tell me what's so urgent that you had to preface it so dramatically," says Kevin.

"Long story short, I'm pregnant," I say.

"Wow! This is great! A child is what I want. I only see this as a blessing! I've been ready for fatherhood for several years, but hadn't found the right woman to share in this experience until I found you," Kevin says.

Kevin and I talk a little bit more and then I leave to go to Eric's house to share the news with him about the pregnancy. He's nervous about the news I have to convey. He probably thinks I want to break up with him again. The last time I told him I needed to talk to him about something, we ended up having sex (unprotected I might add). I use my key to get into Eric's house. He's sitting on the couch enjoying an adult beverage. He hands me an amaretto sour as I sit on the couch, but I don't drink it.

"Baby, I hope you didn't come over to end our relationship," Eric says.

"No honey. I'm not here to end our relationship. I do have some very important news about me though," I reply.

"Well, that's a relief. You had me worrying over here. What's the news you need to share?" Eric asks.

I state, "I'm expecting. I'm having a baby."

"No wonder you didn't sip the drink. You

normally devour them. This calls for a celebration. I am going to be a father! My swimmers work. My boys are going to go crazy!" Eric explains.

I leave Eric to his celebration. I'm tired and want to go home to get in bed. It has been a long day. I feel that I've been a bit misleading. I told Kevin and Eric about my pregnancy, but never actually said that either one of them is the father. I left it for them to assume that they were. I know when the time comes to let one of them know the truth, he will not want to hear anything about I never said he's the father. Oh well, I'll cross that bridge when I come to it. I really don't have a better solution to the problem. The girls and I have already thought this dilemma through and we feel this is the only way to proceed.

Seven months to go before I can put this not knowing behind me. I guess for the time being, I'll have to put up with two men taking care of my every need. It could be worse. I could have no man waiting on me hand and foot. I'm not the first woman to play two men and I won't be the last. I'll enjoy my pregnancy for sure. I have two intelligent, financially stable, and supportive men in my corner. Additionally, I have two of the most helpful and loyal friends walking with me every step of the way.

It's a few weeks later and it's time for my dating ultrasound. Eric and Kevin both want to be involved in every aspect of my pregnancy and

I'm trying hard to minimize their participation. You would think men wouldn't want to be so involved in multiple doctor's visits. The only job I need them to stick to is pampering me and throwing me a little dick when I want it. There are far worse things a girl could complain about, but with them wanting to be in the know so much, they are making this more difficult than I initially anticipated.

I'm telling Kevin one lie and Eric another. Before I know it, I have to make up another lie to support the last lie I told. There is so much to remember. I have to write down the lies that I tell to them in a notebook and study them just to keep up. I don't want to forget what I tell Kevin and Eric and then get my feelings hurt when I get caught up in a lie.

Eric takes me to my dating ultrasound. I had to lie to Kevin to get him to back down about not coming with me. Kevin thinks that Rachel and Ilesha are with me for this appointment. I told him that I promised them that they could attend this appointment. I also promised Kevin that he will definitely be a part of this process and will be included in future appointments. Kevin wasn't very happy about it, but he acquiesced in my decision to make me happy.

I will have to alternate which appointments each of them can go to. I have to ensure that both of them get to equally feel as if they are a part of the process. If Kevin or Eric feels slighted, that may cause some erratic behavior from them. I need them to be even keeled at all times, so I can predict their movements with almost one hundred percent accuracy. This will increase my chances of not getting caught. The appointments that Kevin doesn't make, I'll tell him that the girls are going with me and I'll tell Eric the same thing about the doctor's visits he doesn't attend. Eric and I walk into the doctor's office.

"Good morning. I'm Sheena Mills and I have an appointment this morning," I state.

The lady at the front desk greets me and Eric and he introduces himself as my child's father. He is extremely proud of his future fatherhood. I would be proud too if I had gotten someone as fine as me pregnant. The receptionist seats us briefly. We are only sitting down for about ten minutes when the nurse walks out from the back room and calls my name. Eric and I walk to the back to see the doctor. The visit is very reassuring. The doctor informs us that everything looks good with the pregnancy and that I'm thirteen weeks along. We ask the doctor a few more questions and then we leave.

CHAPTER 11

I am going to have to pull a magic trick out of my ass to keep these two men from finding out my secret. I can't avoid either of them because I'm bearing a child from one of them. It is definitely going to take my "A" game to pull this shit off. Kevin and I just left his office and are heading to his house to chill out for a while. This is a perfect time for us to hang out because Eric is attending meetings and is caught up for the duration of the day. I'm glad because it's pretty stressful wondering if he'll be where I am, especially when I'm with Kevin.

We are driving to Kevin's house through DuPont Circle and my heart drops to my stomach. Eric is in the car sitting right beside us as we come to a stoplight. He's supposed to be in meetings. I thought he would be at the school or at the district office. Damn! I should have found out exactly where he would be, so I wouldn't be in the situation I'm in now. What is he doing out here? Well, it is lunch time. Maybe he's on lunch break or just traveling to another meeting. I hope he doesn't look over here at us. Shit, I hope he hasn't already spotted me.

I wonder if Kevin would roll down the window if Eric summoned him to do so. All I know is that I'm a sitting duck in this car. What will I do if Eric calls? I have no idea. I need to do something to get away from his car.

I state, "I'm not feeling so well. I need to put my seat down. All of a sudden something just came over me. I don't know what it is."

"Babe, do you need me to pull over or something?" Kevin asks.

"No, no. Don't pull over. We are close to your job still. Just head back there for a minute," I reply.

He says, "Okay, cool."

This is not how I envisioned my life being. I'm faking sick to hide from one of my lovers. It's stressful juggling these men, but I must admit that it's a little exhilarating too. Great sex from both of them and some excitement to keep my life interesting. The focus of two men, I'll take it.

We are heading back to Kevin's job when my fears are confirmed.

"I think we are being followed," Kevin says.

"Really? Are you sure?" I ask.

I decide to play dumb and act like I don't

know who could be following us. I pretend like I think he's saying the cops are pulling us over.

I ask, "What do the cops want with us?"

Kevin states, "It's not the police. It's some dude in a white Cadillac."

"Oh my. He could be a maniac or something! I'm scared now," I state.

"No need to be scared. I won't let anything happen to you. He's definitely following us though. Every turn we make, he makes too," Kevin states.

"That's weird. Did you cut him off or something?" I ask.

"I cut him off slightly when I got over to turn around, but it doesn't warrant all of this. I'm about to pull over and see what this idiot wants," says Kevin.

This is typical Kevin. He is so hard on the outside. He never bows down to anyone. I'm surprised his middle name isn't Macho. Now Eric is calling my phone. He saw me for sure and knows that I'm in the car. So much for tinted windows. These two men might fight right here on the street if Kevin pulls over.

I can't let this happen like this. I have to intervene first. I have to manipulate Kevin into getting us out of this situation.

"Hmm, if you wanna play gangster liken to some thug in the streets, then pull over and let me out. I am not letting you put me and my baby in harm's way because of your testosterone," I say.

"You mean our baby," Kevin says.

I state, "I said it right the first time. When you jeopardize me, you lose your parental rights. I just told you that I'm sick and you wanna accost some maniac in the streets. Do better! You need to be getting us out of harm's way," I narrate.

Kevin immediately apologizes for losing his cool and explains he would never think of harming his family. I let him know it's okay, but he does need to do something to get Eric off of our tail.

"I'll drive fast and lose this guy," Kevin says.

I instruct Kevin to drive past the police department instead of weaving in and out of traffic like he's a NASCAR driver. He follows my suggestion and goes to the nearest police department. As we pull up by the station, a cop is coming out. Kevin stops the car and informs the cop that the Cadillac behind us is following us.

The cop immediately tells Eric to stop and he complies. Kevin wants to get out of the car and see what the deal is.

"Kevin, if you get out, the cops are gonna take down your info and his. It'll be a big scene and paperwork. On top of that, the manic will know your name and potentially where to find you. I think we should keep going," I narrate.

"You don't feel well anyway. Bottom line is he can't follow us since the police officer has him stopped," Kevin says.

Kevin drives away as I urge him to do.

"Exactly, take me home," I say.

All this action has gotten me a little revved up and in a freaky mood. I grab Kevin's dick through his pants as we drive home. I zip his pants down and pull his dick out. I stroke it until it's bulging hard. I begin sucking it as he turns corners on the way back to my house. He rubs my hair and begins gyrating with every sucking motion. I know it's hard for him to concentrate on driving, but it turns me on even more seeing him trying to fight the sensation. I give more attention to the head and Kevin begins to squirm and lets out a soft whimper as he eventually cums.

I know he needed to bust a nut. If I wouldn't have given him head, he would've wanted to come in the house to get some. Now since he's released, I know he will be quick to leave once he drops me off. Men don't really like to stick around after they bust a nut and I know that. I need him gone as quickly as possible. Just as I figure it, Kevin offers no objection when I tell him I'm going to sleep and will contact him later. I really would've wanted him to stay, but it's likely that Eric is heading over.

I don't want Eric to come to the house after the cops let him go and catch Kevin here. Just as I predicted, as soon as Kevin leaves, Eric pulls up. He has been calling over and over again. I finally answer the phone with a voice that makes it seem like I've been sleeping.

"What you up to?" Eric asks.

"I'm in the bed. Not feeling well today," I respond.

"I'm in front of your house. I don't see your car," Eric says.

"I don't know why it's not out there. It should be. You're more worried about the car than me. You didn't even comment on my illness," I voice.

"If you're home, then open the door. Like I said, I'm outside," Eric mentions.

"You seem a little hostile. I'm coming downstairs now," I reply.

I greet Eric warmly with a kiss on the lips. I hope he isn't able to taste any of Kevin's nut on my lips. Eric is visibly disturbed. He's about to flip on me, but I have a trick for him. He's not ready for my wits.

"How were your meetings?" I ask.

Eric begins to tell me about his day. The meetings he had didn't last all day because there was some conflict with the superintendent. All of the principals think their boss is being unreasonable with his expectations. This tension and arguing ended the meetings early. Then he explains that somebody cut him off in traffic. He was so upset that he followed the car and that it looked a lot like Rachel's car. During the pursuit of the car that cut him off, he was stopped by the cops. He informs me that he only called me the number of times he did because he wanted to unload some of his frustrations. He's extremely happy that he didn't get in trouble with the cops.

"Why didn't you get in trouble?" I ask.

He replies, "The car I was following just pulled off after the cops stopped me. I got lucky because I was vexed about him cutting me off. It was just a pile up of the day's events. I was wrong. The cop talked to me for a minute or two and let me go."

I did all that worrying for nothing. He never saw me in the car. I guess it worked out that I proceeded as if he knew I was in the vehicle. If I would've let Kevin stay, it would be chaotic for me now for sure.

"Sorry, you had such a poor day. I wish I could've helped. I've just been so drained today. Leaving the house requires energy that I don't have," I say.

"No, it's cool. I just want the woman carrying my offspring to be well. You need to call the cops about your car. It's not outside," says Eric.

I respond, "Man, I'm tripping. The car is in the garage. I was so out of it, that I forgot that I parked in the garage. My fault."

I knew the car was in the garage the entire time. It's just a strategy I use on Eric and Kevin. I can't afford for them to know exactly when I'm home, so I park in the garage sometimes and other times I don't. In some instances I park in the driveway, but I'm not home at all. I like to keep them off balance to allow myself more wiggle room. They can never really tell when I'm home and when I'm not. I even have my girls take my car while I'm home chilling out. I use whatever diversions necessary to not get caught.

I don't see how men keep up double lives for months or even years at a time. It takes a certain level of patience and guile to keep up a front for so long. I don't see how they have the energy to do it. I'm only a few months into my scam and I'm almost ready to call it quits. It's too time consuming, bothersome, and expensive. I have to admit that I do play the part very well. I make sure I treat each of my men as if he is the only man in my life. Luckily for me, there's an end to this madness.

CHAPTER 12

It's week sixteen and this pregnancy can't be over quickly enough. I'm on my way to the doctor for my scheduled sonogram to find out the sex of the baby. The girls are interested in knowing if I'm having a girl or a boy because they feel knowing will help them to better prepare. I, on the other hand, don't really care if I'm having a boy or a girl. I'm more concerned with having a healthy baby without any complications. Please let this be a breeze. The girls are riding to the doctor with me. I didn't want them to come, but they would not have it any other way. I guess some girls' company doesn't hurt. Besides, when I told Kevin and Eric about the sonogram they both wanted to come. I obviously cut that short.

We arrive at the doctor's office at my scheduled appointment time. The girls come in the examination room with me. We are all excited about the soon-to-be new addition to our family. The doctor puts some jelly on my stomach and moves the transducer over my skin.

The doctor states, "Well, Sheena it appears that you are having a boy."

Rachel says, "He is going to be so cute. We'll dress him up in little suits and take him to church. He'll be raised to be respectful and honest."

"I can handle a little boy. I hope I don't spoil him rotten," I say.

"Let's face it; he's going to get spoiled by us and his father. You know how men are about their sons. They feel like they have an heir to their throne or something," explains Ilesha.

The doctor finishes up and exits the room while I clean up.

"It is still going to be interesting when one of those poor men finds out he doesn't have a son even though he thinks he does. Girl, I don't want to be you," Rachel remarks.

"One of them is going to flip. What you have to bear is just too much," says Ilesha.

"Yeah, I know. I'm trying not to think about it. It's crazy the way life throws us unthinkable twists," I reply. "Please take me home. I'm tired."

It seems like only days since my sonogram, but it's been four weeks. I'm getting huge. My stomach is poking out further and further each day. I'm still working and trying to maintain my personal affairs as I normally do. My face is full and my nose is even fuller. I love being pregnant, but I don't like some of the things that come along with it like my skin discoloration and unpredictable appetite. My girls have bought me many fashionable maternity outfits, so I still feel cute to some degree. I wonder if I'll ever be able to get my perfect figure back. I'll do my best to get rid of all of this extra weight I'm carrying.

I feel my bundle of joy moving inside of me. I don't feel strong kicks, but more like small nudges or pokes. It's his way of communicating with me. I feel at one with my son. I wish I could tap him back, but I can't. I normally just rub my stomach and talk to him for a minute or two.

"Mommy feels you baby. I'm here and I love you very much," I say all the time.

I'm not sure if he can hear me, but it makes me feel better to speak a few words to him. He moves so much inside of me. As Rachel, Ilesha, and I are sitting here conversing, he's nudging me now.

"Ooh girl, here he goes again. He has been at it all day long. I hope everything's okay," I say.

Ilesha states, "Let me feel your stomach. Oh yeah, I feel him in there. It's probably nothing. He is a boy and you know how rough and rambunctious boys can be. You are gonna have an active one, it seems."

Rachel places her hand on my stomach too. Now we are all sharing with my son's communication with the world. This is a special moment for me because it's symbolic of how his life will be. We will all have a hand in raising my little boy.

Rachel states, "I feel a lot of movement in there. It's almost like there is more than one baby. That's a lot of movement simultaneously for one child."

As we feel around a little more, we all agree that there's seemingly more movement than one child could be responsible for. We are all a bit shocked by the possibility of twins.

"If I'm carrying twins, the doctor would have let me know weeks ago when I went for the sonogram," I say.

Ilesha responds, "Not necessarily, in many instances one baby is hidden by the other one. This could be the case."

"I've heard of this many times. In fact, my friend Tammy experienced the same thing during her pregnancy some years ago. Not to mention, twins do run in your family. It may be your turn for twins," explains Rachel.

"Twins skip a generation in some instances, but not always," says Ilesha.

"Well, I need to know as soon as possible. I'm going to the doctor. Hopefully, he will be able to see my other child if he or she is in there," I state.

"Are you going to tell the potential fathers?" asks Rachel.

"Don't tell them anything. They don't need to

know anything just yet," says Ilesha.

"I'm meeting up with Eric later, but I'm not going to mention anything about the possibility of twins. I won't say anything until it's confirmed," I say.

"True, that makes sense. There may not be anything to tell him or Kevin anyway," says Rachel.

"In fact, fooling around with you two, I almost forgot I'm meeting Eric in twenty minutes. Let me go. I'll call the doctor while I'm on my way to meet him," I say.

I call the doctor as I drive to meet Eric. I tell the doctor my suspicions and he tells me to come in for another ultrasound a week from today. I'm okay with that. It's not like having twins is a life or death situation. The only thing that will change if I'm having twins is the number of things I have to buy. It's going to pretty much double everything.

I walk into the restaurant and see where Eric is seated. He's looking better every day and I'm the opposite. Well, at least I feel that way. I wonder if he thinks I'm bad looking in my pregnancy. Oh well, I can't change it right now, but I will bounce back from this. His chocolate skin has not a blemish on it. He's making me look bad.

"You are a stunning pregnant woman," Eric says as he pulls out a seat for me to sit down.

"Thank you. You always make me smile. I needed that compliment. Not really feeling my sharpest right now," I say.

Eric and I talk about the baby and many other things. About thirty minutes later I see one of Eric's friends walking through the restaurant. Eric summons him over to us. Moments later, Rachel and Ilesha walk into the restaurant. I focus my attention on them as they approach our table. I'm confused about why our friends are randomly appearing at the eatery. When I turn around, Eric is down on one knee with a jewelry box in his hand.

"Sheena, you are the woman of my dreams. I want to live a thousand lifetimes waking up next to you. My life's quest will be to make you and our child happier than words can describe," Eric narrates.

At this point of his speech and him being on one knee, I know where he is headed with his words. I never wanted to have children out of wedlock and he's about to keep that from happening.

He asks, "Will you make me a complete person and marry me?"

I'm sitting here knowing what I know about my pregnancy and he's asking me for my hand in marriage. Marriage? Marriage is based on honesty and trust. I don't know how I should answer. Rachel and Ilesha are both looking at me in awe. They know what I know and can feel my pain. What should I do? Should I say yes or no? Can I really say no with this grand audience and setup in this restaurant? He'll be devastated if I say no. Is there a clever way I can give myself more time to answer his question?

I can't believe the quandary I've created. This is the type of stuff that gets people killed. If I say yes, I'll be engaged to this man and potentially carrying someone else's child. I know he's only asking me to marry him because he thinks the child is his. He doesn't even know that he loves me under false pretenses. I'm not going to accept his proposal. I'll tell him the truth and get from under this tremendous amount of pressure. He may be upset, but at least I'll be able to sleep better at night. I don't need this stress in my life, and I definitely don't need it while carrying my baby.

Can I truly say no to a marriage proposal from a man who I love? Does it really make sense to turn him down when I genuinely love him? I never thought it was possible to be in love with two men at the same time, but I now know from my current situation that it's feasible. I may not get another opportunity to be married. Some women never get married or end up settling for someone they aren't in love with.

I wish Rachel would give me a signal, so I will know what to do. She's the level headed one in the crew and gives the most sound advice. Can I get a head nod from her or a signal of some sort? This is crazy that they are standing here with me, but I have never felt more alone in my entire life.

I know Rachel wouldn't want me to hurt this man's feelings in front of everyone. My mind is racing a thousand miles per second. Everybody is waiting for me to answer his question.

I ask, "Why me?"

"Because I see the good in you. I love your determination, your spirit, and I love the way I feel when we are together. It's like the world is at peace and nothing else matters. I love you and I am in love with you," Eric narrates.

The ring he presents me with is huge. The bling is perfect and I absolutely love it. It's like he read my mind because this is exactly the type of ring I would've picked out myself. It's kind of weird. The ring I always dreamed of being presented with, looks eerily similar to this one. How could he be so spot on with his choice?

His words are sincere and moving. He's been very articulate since the first time I met him. His warm soothing words have me weak in the knees. His oratory skills remind me of Dr. Martin Luther King Jr.'s speaking abilities because they are very impactful. He makes me want to jump into his arms right now and scream "Yes" while he whisks me away. I can see the sincerity in his eyes and hear the heartfelt tone of his voice. He is all about me, but I'm not all about him. He shares me with Kevin. What is a girl to do? All I can do is go for mine. You only live once!

As I tremble with extreme happiness I say, "Yes, Eric. I will marry you!"

By now the audience watching is applauding. Everyone is overcome with joy. My face is moist from the tears of elation. I'm afforded much gratification knowing that someone thinks enough of me to ask to spend the rest of his life with me. I'm also relieved because I'm finally engaged. Each year I age, I would always wonder if it would ever happen and it finally has. I feel like a two ton weight has been lifted from my shoulders. Eric slips the ring on my finger and plants an endearing kiss on my lips. We are now having an improvised engagement party at the restaurant. My girls make their way over to me to congratulate me, but I also know they want to talk to me just as much as I want to talk to them.

"Congratulations girl! We are so happy for you," Ilesha and Rachel say.

"Thanks girls! I appreciate it. I'm pregnant and engaged at the same time. I never saw this coming," I say.

We walk away from the rest of the people in the restaurant, so we can talk privately.

I say, "I'm so happy and confused at the same time. I didn't know what to do, so I went with yes. I mean, I do love him."

"You handled that as well as you could have. I was stunned when he dropped down on his knee," Rachel says. "Eric contacted us on Facebook and told us to come down here."

"Girl, that was some crazy shit that popped off! I almost lost it. I know you are going through it right now," says Ilesha. "We would have told you if we knew. Eric told us that it was going to be a surprise pregnancy party."

"Do you think you will go through with the marriage?" asks Rachel.

I say, "I don't know what I'm going to do. I'm in love with two men simultaneously. I'm pregnant by one of them and engaged to one of them. I have a lot to contend with."

"As always, we will be here with you every step of the way," Rachel says.

I know they will. That's the only thing that's certain in my life right now. It seems that everything else is up in the air. I'm trying not to stress over everything that's going on. For now, I'll put the wedding plans on the back burner. I need to find out if I'm having twins and do whatever I need to do to have a healthy pregnancy.

I've been engaged for several days and today is the day I have my appointment with the doctor. I'm sitting in the lobby waiting for someone to call me to the back. Kevin is here with me. He feels like he hasn't been an active participant in the process. He's jealous of the girls because I allow them to come along for everything. He wouldn't take "no" for an answer this time. It's cool because he does need to be in the know. I had to tell Eric a couple of lies to keep him away from the doctor's office.

The nurse calls me to the back to see if my

suspicion of twins is ill founded. As she leads Kevin and me to the examination room, she looks back at me and says, "I see you brought your brother with you today. He's very handsome."

I think all of the blood has left my face and all of the air has escaped my lungs.

I'm standing there speechless as Kevin chimes in curtly, "I'm not her brother. I'm the father-to-be."

The nurse looks at me momentarily with confusion on her face. At that moment, I'm sure she remembers Eric from my dating ultrasound. I was hoping enough time had passed that the staff wouldn't remember. She motions us into the room and I enter while trying to avoid any additional eye contact. I can feel her judgmental eyes piercing the back of my head.

"The doctor will be with you shortly," she states and closes the door.

The doctor enters about ten minutes later. He explains the first test he's going to run is a test to check for multiple heartbeats in my stomach. He uses the fetal Doppler to perform the test. After a quick test, he confirms the presence of two heartbeats. He feels very confident that I'm having twins. He also takes another ultrasound to see if the other baby can be seen. This time my second baby boy is making his presence known. We can see both of them now.

I ask the doctor, "Is it normal for one of the

babies to be hidden?"

"Yes, it's normal. In some instances one baby blocks the other. That was the case in your last sonogram. Nothing to worry about. All signs point to two healthy baby boys," he replies.

"How do you feel about twins Kevin?" I ask.

"I feel fine. I think we are in great shape to raise two kids. It's even better for them because they will grow up together. They'll have a best friend from the very beginning. I believe strongly that siblings need to grow up together. It helps to keep the family strong. The next generation will have a healthy sense of family," Kevin explains.

I agree with what he's saying. Kids being close to one another can help keep future generations of the family from getting watered down and separated. Kevin drives me home, while I text Rachel, Ilesha, and Eric to tell them the news. They are all excited about the news. I don't know if I'm tired because I'm just tired or if the news of having twins has tired me out. I want Kevin and his red-boned self to come inside to give me some, but I'm worn out. He won't be getting any today.

CHAPTER 13

Eric's birthday is almost here. I can't believe how quickly the time has passed. I guess with all of the running, ducking, and hiding I've been doing, time has gotten away from me. Not to mention, I am pregnant. I have a surprise party in the making for him. Friday night is going to be very special. I know he'll be completely surprised when he walks into the venue. I'll spend some time on Thursday and early Friday to set the place up. The girls and I have already been shopping, so I have the perfect after-hours accessories for Eric's "dessert" after the party.

I've already informed Kevin that I'll be working on a project for my business and will be busy trying to finish up on Thursday and entertaining clients on Friday.

Thursday arrives and I text Kevin to see if he's available for lunch. I want to get some quality time in with him before I get too involved with the duties of Eric's party. If I don't see him today, I won't have the opportunity to see him again until Saturday at the earliest. Fortunately, Kevin accepts my lunch invitation.

I meet Kevin at a local bar and grill. We eat and talk. I'm picking Kevin's brain to see what plans he has for tomorrow. I hope he's busy. If he is, he really won't be concerned about me.

I ask, "What are you doing this weekend?"

Kevin replies, "I'm not sure. One of my boys is talking about coming over and watching the game, but nothing's solidified."

"Guys' night in! Sounds like some female stuff to me," I reply.

"Oh, so you're a comedian now? I'll let you get that," Kevin states.

"You didn't let me get that. I took that. Thank you very much!" I retort.

"I have a right hook with your name on it! You know I can deliver it too," Kevin says.

We both laugh and I let him know that Lorena Bobbitt is a good friend of mine and I taught her everything she knows. I love joking back and forth with Kevin like this. Lunch is seemingly over before I know it. They say time flies when you're having fun. It's definitely true in this circumstance. Sometimes the guilt of what I'm doing makes me want to come clean, but I have to see this through. Maybe I'm selfish, but no one's perfect.

The party is upon us now. Many guests have already arrived and plenty more are filing in. I'm glad that there is such a good turnout. You know how it goes. People say they're going to show up, but don't. Fortunately, that's not the case tonight. Eric is on his way and should be here any minute. I told him that I was working here at the Diamond Center and wanted him to accompany me. He will be stunned when he notices all of his friends are here. He's been working a lot of long hours lately, so this will be a great way for him to unwind. Eric is calling me now. I told him to call me when he arrived, so I could escort him in.

"Hi baby. I'm outside," Eric says.

I reply, "Hey, I'm walking to the front now. Thanks for coming. It means a lot."

I walk to the front to meet Eric. He's looking very dapper as always.

As we walk into the ballroom, everyone screams, "Happy Birthday!"

Eric's face is filled with shock, but it's a good type of shock. He grabs me close and gives me a kiss on the lips.

"Thank you, honey. This is a total surprise, I must say. And thank all of you for coming out tonight," Eric states.

All of his friends greet him and the night is going smoothly. Eric is telling everyone how he had no idea I was planning a surprise for him. He even reports that he was slightly upset that I had him attending a work function on his birthday. Well technically his birthday starts at midnight, but I figured he'd be expecting something if I put this together on his birthday. This way is better because he will bring in his birthday by celebrating with his family and closest friends.

Eric is mingling with his friends and colleagues, so I go sit my pregnant ass down. I've been on my feet all day. I'm glad Eric isn't much of a dancer because I don't think I can hang tonight.

Just as I'm in a position to relax, the unthinkable happens. *No fucking way! This can't be happening!*

Kevin! What the fuck is Kevin doing in here?! Who is that guy he's with? There is no way in hell Kevin knows Eric. At least I hope not. Eric will be livid if he finds out that me, the woman who's possibly carrying his child, his fiancée, is cheating on him. That bad news would be devastating if he finds out here, at his birthday party, in front of all of his friends and family. It's a small damn world. As big as D.C. is, I would never imagine Kevin and Eric would end up in the same building at the same time.

I hope he doesn't see me. Kevin is taking off his jacket and sitting down. He's definitely here to stay for a while. He told me he was staying in to watch the game. I can't be bothered with what he was supposed to be doing. The bottom line is that he's here now. I recognize one of the guys he came in with as his cousin. I can't say I recognize the other guy. The unknown gentleman he came in with is talking to Eric now. Just my fucking luck. Kevin's friend is obviously a friend of Eric.

I can't risk Eric attempting to introduce me to his friend and by default he introduces me to Kevin. I have to leave immediately. No, I have to hide. I don't know what I have to do. Why is Kevin coming this way? I'm going to the back room and I am not leaving it.

I can see the entire ballroom from my spot in the back room. Kevin stops at the bar and then Eric walks over to the bar too. My stomach is in my ass. From what I can see, they're not talking to each other. It only takes one word to start up a conversation and then it could be over. I have to get Kevin out of here right now! What the hell can I do?

I text Eric and tell him that I'm in the bathroom, so he doesn't come looking for me. I call Ilesha to see if I can get some emergency assistance. I only see this ending badly if I don't get some help fast.

"Hey girl! I am so screwed right now!" I yell.

"What's the deal and why are you screaming?" asks Ilesha.

"Kevin just walked his ass into Eric's birthday party," I report.

"Get the fuck outta here! That's a bitch! You

gotta be kidding me! What are you going to do?" she asks.

"Yeah, I'm sick to my stomach. To make matters worse, they are standing on line next to one another at the bar. I need an intervention," I say in a panicked fashion.

"Girl! I can't believe they know each other!" states Ilesha.

I reply, "It doesn't appear that they know each other. Kevin came in with his cousin and another guy. It looks like Eric knows the nondescript guy. Eric and Kevin just happen to be at the bar at the same time. I don't want them to start talking and put two and two together."

"I feel you girl! You have to get a plan together, right now!" Ilesha states.

"I know. I know. I need you and Rachel to make it work though," I state.

I tell Ilesha the details of the plan. She agrees to help me. I see Kevin and Eric are beginning to converse. I know I have to put that conversation to rest immediately. It's time to put "operation separation" into effect. Ilesha and I proceed with the plan. I tell Ilesha to conference call Kevin and let me speak. I see Kevin look at his phone screen with a slight look of confusion. He excuses himself from Eric and answers the call.

"Hi, Ilesha. I didn't expect to see your name flashing on my screen," Kevin says.

"Babe it's me, Sheena. I'm calling from Ilesha's phone because mine went dead. I need a big favor," I say.

He replies, "I was wondering why your friend would be calling me at all, but especially at night."

I say, "I know you were looking at the phone wondering why she's calling you. That's funny. I hope you aren't too caught up in your football game because we have a flat tire. We were going to pick up some extra stuff for my work function and the tire blew out. I don't know what to do. I have to get back to this function immediately."

He replies, "I didn't even watch the game. Me, my cousin, and one of his boys ended up at a party, but that doesn't matter. I'm leaving now."

I see Kevin, his cousin, and his friend walking out of the Diamond Center. As we continue to talk on the phone, I tell Kevin that we are on the other side of town. I send him in the direction that Ilesha is nearest. I need to ensure that she gets there before he does. That will also give Ilesha time to pick Rachel up.

I'm relieved that phase one of my plan is working. Kevin is in his car and heading to meet us. I can relax a little bit now that Rachel and Ilesha have made it to the fictitious break down location and Kevin is out of the building. Kevin arrives shortly after my girls do. He expects to see me, but I'm not there, of course. Ilesha and Rachel have been instructed to call me as soon as Kevin pulls up. I'm on the phone when I hear Kevin pulling up and asking where I am.

Rachel quickly hands Kevin the phone. She is

not very comfortable with lying, even though she's very good at it. Fortunately, she uses her powers for good. Kevin takes the phone.

I say, "Hi, honey. I'm glad you came. I really appreciate it."

He says, "Don't mention it. I'm glad I can help. I thought you were stranded with them."

"I was, but I needed to get back here as soon as possible. Coincidentally, a taxi was driving past right after I talked to you, so I jumped in it. It didn't make sense to wait for you to get there, change the tire, and then bring us back here. Too much time would have passed," I explain.

"Gotcha. I feel you on that. It seems like things always go wrong at the worst possible moment," he says.

"You already know. I was going to call you and tell you as soon as I got in the cab, but Rachel called me to make sure the cab driver didn't kidnap me. I took Ilesha's phone with me since mine is dead. I hope it's just the battery. These phones aren't any good these days," I say.

"Speak for your beat up phone. My phone is fine and hasn't given me any problems," Kevin says.

"Well Babe, thanks again. I gotta get back in here, so let me go," I say.

Kevin states, "Alright, enjoy the rest of the night. Don't work too hard. Me and my boys will have this tire changed in no time. Been changing tires since I was a little boy. Talk to you later."

Kevin hangs up the phone. I don't anticipate him coming back to the party after changing a tire. I walk back into the banquet room where Eric's party is being held. He is probably wondering what's taking me so long to return. I couldn't come back out here until I had this situation under control. I walk over to Eric.

"Did you miss me?" I ask.

"Nah, I didn't. I didn't realize you were gone. I thought you were still beside me," Eric says.

"Boy, whatever! You know you missed me. Trying to play me. I see how you do. That was a good one. Maybe you won't miss me when I step off," I say as I turn to walk away.

Eric grabs my hand and says, "You ain't going nowhere, so I'm not worried."

"I don't know about that. According to you, you wouldn't notice I was even gone," I retort.

Eric lets out a light chuckle. A slow song comes on and Eric and I hit the dance floor. I'm still moving pretty good for a pregnant woman. Most females at my stage of pregnancy would be home in bed, but not me. I'm an active and pretty good looking pregnant woman. Kevin and Eric both tell me all the time how gorgeous I am. We mingle and dance until all of the guests leave the party. We leave the Diamond Center around two in the morning. We head straight to Eric's house for a mind blowing session of dirty talk and rough sex. All I can think of is how this night almost ended in tragedy. I never expected to be going through so much drama during my pregnancy.

CHAPTER 14

It's two days before my due date and I'm ready to give birth to my baby boys. I almost want to go to the doctor today and have my babies delivered now. Everything's in place for my sons. I have the nursery set up and the girls threw me a baby shower that was out of this world. I received many gifts that will help me with the boys. I have more things for them than I know what to do with. I'm sure they will all come in handy at some point.

I have no idea how I am going to keep Kevin and Eric out of the delivery room. That's one reason why I want to have these babies today. If I have the babies today or tomorrow, I'll be in great shape because Kevin is out of town working. He plans to be back on my due date. Both Kevin and Eric are pretty adamant about being there for the birth of their first child. I really want my girls in the delivery room with me. They will be more comforting than either one of them. Plus, if Kevin is in the delivery room, I will be on edge knowing that Eric could pop up at any moment or vice versa.

Ilesha and Rachel are here at the house with me acting like they are my maids. I really appreciate them. They are more nurturing and comforting than my fiancé and boyfriend. I can't believe that I have a fiancé and a boyfriend. I have myself in such a mess and I keep replaying the events in my head that got me here. Oh how I wanted a man, a wonderful relationship, and eventually a family. This is such a tangled web that I hope will soon be over.

"Girl, we are gonna have to get you in the gym as soon as possible because you can't lose your figure," Ilesha says.

Rachel states, "Most definitely. We are going to have stick to a tight workout schedule for sure. I always used your figure as motivation for me in the gym."

"Thanks girls! You two will be envious of my figure again. Wait and see. You know I'm a fitness guru. I will be your inspiration once again," I narrate.

Ilesha states, "You have a hell of a mountain to climb because your stomach is huge girl! There may be more than two loaves of bread in your oven!"

We all laugh at her joke of me. I have been

blessed with a fairly simple pregnancy. There have been no major hang ups. My biggest issue is all of the weight I've gained. I know that having a flat stomach is a goal that will be hard to reach, but I can get it back. My cousin, Ann, had four children and got back to her small size. If she can do it, so can I. I remember her getting her kids to help her workout. My boys will be too young, but my girls are up for it. I'll even get Eric or Kevin to assist with my up keep.

"Help me up girls. I have to tinkle," I say.

Ilesha and Rachel help me up and I hurry to the bathroom. This sensation to urinate is stronger than ever. I hope I can make it to the bathroom.

"Damn it!" I yell.

Rachel and Ilesha hurry over to me and ask, "What's wrong?"

"I couldn't hold it. I just wet myself and it's all over the floor," I say.

"Um girl, I don't think that's urine. Your water just broke," says Ilesha.

"This is it! It's that time!" I say.

"You need to call your doctor and see what he advises," says Rachel.

I call my doctor and he informs me that I should proceed to the hospital, so they can make sure everything's in order. He states that he will be inducing my labor and I should be a mom very soon. My girls drive me to the hospital after we pack up everything I may need. I know I should be focused on giving birth, but I can't help but think how lucky I am that Kevin is out of town. I had Ilesha call Eric and tell him what's going on and where to meet us. Ilesha or Rachel will call Kevin sometime tomorrow to let him know that my water broke. I don't want Kevin to have enough time to get back to town. The longer he's gone, the better. He may not be the father anyway.

We arrive at the hospital and they immediately admit me. The doctor talks to me and tells me the procedures for inducing labor. He explains the potential harms for waiting and asks me how I want to proceed. I tell him I'm all for inducing labor. He tells me that it could take a few or many hours depending on how I respond to the medication.

The doctor has given me the medication needed to induce labor. The waiting game begins. Ilesha, Rachel, and Eric are all in here with me. We're all chatting and expressing our excitement. Kevin keeps texting and calling me. I don't want to respond because then I'll have to come clean about where I am. It's better for me to not answer and have the babies. I can always tell him that one of the girls had my phone and that I was in too much pain or something to call. He will have to find solace in that explanation. It is called labor for a reason.

I'm experiencing some serious contractions. The doctor told me they may be more painful because of the induction. After several hours, I am the proud mother of two healthy and handsome little boys. I had a natural vaginal delivery. Eric might need a new hand because I squeezed his hand as hard as I could to relieve some of the pressure off of me. I don't know if it really worked, but squeezing his hand took my mind off of my pain. I'm exhausted and a bit groggy from the pain medicine. I'm in and out of consciousness.

Ilesha has my phone and says that Kevin has not let up on his phone calls. She checks the messages for me and he assumes that I've gone into labor since I haven't returned his texts or phone calls. His last message states that he's flying back to D.C. to be with me during the delivery. Ilesha keeps calling him back, but he's not answering his phone. This is the last thing I need. He can't come back early and come to the hospital. It's like this web of lies is tightening around my neck. I can barely breathe. The thought of getting caught up is suffocating. I'm almost to the finish line and I can't afford for it to all come crashing down. Eric is in la-la land and is completely oblivious of how precarious of a situation he's in.

Rachel, Ilesha, and I all have the same concerns about my two new additions to the family. We still have the issue of paternity to resolve. As we begin to discuss our concerns, Eric walks back into the room and we switch our topic of conversation. I hope the doctor releases me. I don't know if Kevin jumped on a flight or not. I feel bad about not having him in the loop. He doesn't deserve this. Eric needs to get out of here, so me and the girls can talk.

"Eric, this hospital food is not agreeing with me. I need you to go get me a salad from The Salad Bar. You know how much I love their salads," I say.

"That's cool. Nothing is too much for the mother of my children. Let me know if you think of something else you need while I'm out," he says.

"Now that he's gone we need to get this all worked out. We have to put something in place to make sure this doesn't blow up at the hospital. I can't believe that I'm scheming on my kids' birthday," I say.

Rachel has the DNA kit to send off to the lab. She's going to swab the twin's mouths for a DNA samples. We already have Kevin and Eric's samples. Rachel has to drop off the samples at the lab for testing. I have to pay extra money to get the results back in three days. I would pay three times that amount if I could get the results sooner. This will undoubtedly be the longest three days of my life. Just in case Kevin ends up in town, we've come up with a plan to keep him at bay.

Rachel gets the DNA samples from the boys and leaves for the night. She has to get to the lab as early as possible. The sooner they get the samples, the better. Ilesha stays with me, so she can handle my phone if Kevin calls. As luck would have it, he calls again.

His message states that he's back in town and for me to call him as soon as I can. He also states that he is going to stop by my house.

That is perfect. I need him to be occupied for as much time as possible. It's a definite that he'll call the hospitals looking for me. Ilesha told the hospital staff that someone may be looking for me to cause harm. The hospital staff agreed not to release any patient information about me. They will tell anyone who calls looking for me that they don't have a patient by my name.

I can sleep a little bit better knowing that the likelihood of Kevin showing up is slim to none. The only problem now is he may be at my house when we pull up from leaving here. The doctor says he will be releasing me and the boys tomorrow unless something changes adversely. I feel like a sitting duck here, so leaving will be a good thing. Eric brought my salad back to the hospital and goes home for the night.

It's the next morning and the doctor is releasing us. Eric comes back to check on us and to take us home. The last thing I need is for him to take us home because Kevin sent a text letting me know that he was going to wait outside of my place until he heard something otherwise. Ilesha sends Eric to get his car and Ilesha calls Kevin from my phone. She tells Kevin that I've delivered the babies and I'm in the hospital. She tells him that they are in the process of releasing me and that I will be home at noon.

I'll be home long before noon, but she wants us to have time just in case we can't get rid of Eric in a timely manner. She also tells Kevin some things I need from various stores to get him away from the house. I will explain all of the other stuff to him later. He agrees to get the necessities for me. I'm released from the hospital and Eric drives us home while Ilesha follows.

She's a lifesaver. There is no way I could have pulled this off without her devious mind. Eric and Ilesha get us settled in the house. I head straight for the shower. I send Eric home and Ilesha stays with me until Kevin arrives. Kevin apologizes for not being present for the birth. He never mentions not being able to find where we were. I guess it doesn't really matter. He's concerned with me and the boys. Ilesha is in the living room about to leave when she hears a car pull up. Eric is back at the house. We have no idea why he would be back because he just left.

Fortunately, Ilesha is able to get outside before he rings the doorbell.

"What's up Eric? Is everything alright?" Ilesha asks.

"I forgot my wallet in the diaper bag. I had all that stuff in my hand and just tossed it in there. I'll run in and get it," Eric explains.

177

"Well, she's in there with Rachel. Sheena is having a female moment, so I don't think you should go in there. In fact, I'll get it," Ilesha says.

"Oh okay. I know how private women are during those 'female moments'. Rachel's car is nice. I liked this car ever since I saw it when y'all had girls' night," says Eric.

"Yeah, it's her car and it's nice, but let me grab that wallet for you," Ilesha says.

"Nah, I'll grab it. I know exactly where it is. It's right by the door in the bag," says Eric.

Eric runs up the outdoor steps and enters the house. He's rummaging through the diaper bag in the living room, while Kevin is in the nursery with the boys. If he hears Kevin upstairs, there's going to be drama in here today.

Ilesha walks into the house and snatches the bag and takes it outside. Once out of the house, she scolds Eric for not respecting a female's privacy. She's playing the part like a veteran actress. She gives Eric his wallet. Eric apologizes and drives off.

It's Monday and the results of the DNA tests are ready for pickup. Me and the girls load the kids up and go pick up the results. I don't open the results of the test until we make it back to my house. I put the boys to bed and then head downstairs to the living room to open the test results. I really want a drink to calm my nerves, but can't because I am breastfeeding.

Rachel asks, "So what do you think?"

I respond, "I'm hoping for the best is all I can say."

"A hundred bucks says it's Kevin," Ilesha remarks.

I open the results of the test and the results are mind boggling.

"This can't be right," I say.

Rachel and Ilesha both look at the paternity test results and can't believe what they are reading either.

"Somebody at the lab clearly made a mistake, so they will have to test them again and at no charge to you! Can anybody do their job without screwing up?" asks Rachel.

I call the lab to talk to the lab technician about how the test results were messed up. The results of the test indicate that Eric is the father of one of my sons and Kevin is the father of my other child. The girls and I noticed the distinction in their skin complexions, but it's not abnormal for fraternal twins to not look alike. One of my sons is light skinned like Kevin and the other is brown skinned which is Eric's complexion.

The technician explains that they stand behind their test results. He also explains that it's possible for a woman to become impregnated by two men at one time. He tells me that women sometimes release two eggs during ovulation. He then says that if a woman is sexually active with two men within days of one another, each man could potentially fertilize each egg with his sperm.

What he described is exactly what I did. I slept with Kevin and Eric on back to back days and they both ejaculated inside of me. Twins run in my family, so it is likely that I released two eggs at once. This explains why both my sons look totally different.

"Girls, what am I going to do now?" I ask.

"It may be time to come clean. The lies have to stop at some point," says Rachel.

"No girl, don't tell them. We can think of something. Let's just brainstorm this one like we always do," says Ilesha.

Rachel explains, "Ilesha, she can't lie to both of them forever about their kid. Even if she lies to them further and isn't caught, the kids will get older and understand that two men are coming around saying that he's their father. They will want to know who their father is and they definitely deserve the truth."

"Thanks girls. I will take your advice into consideration as I always do. This one will be interesting. My boys will need their fathers in their lives. I will figure something out," I say.

CHAPTER 15

Another week has gone by and I have not informed Kevin or Eric about the results of the paternity tests. I am so afraid of what they will say to me when I tell them the truth. I also know they will think I'm a conniving whore, but I am so not that. I am simply a woman who fell in love with two men at the same damn time. I never wanted to be in this situation. I only wanted one man to sweep me off my feet. I never would've done this on purpose. I'm still engaged to Eric, but I know he will rescind his proposal once I come clean.

I've been thinking long and hard about my situation and what I should do. A minute doesn't pass where this isn't weighing on my mind. One minute I want to confess and the next minute I'm coming up with another lie to cover all of the other lies I've told. I've already lost seven pounds and I haven't even been working out. I know it's from the stress I'm under. I don't eat and I can barely sleep. The boys are definitely keeping me busy as well. Between feedings and changing diapers, you would think I wouldn't have time to worry about anything else. One good thing is I'm getting my figure back and I'm sure breastfeeding two babies is also a huge help.

I know exactly what I am going to do, but I'm going to lose big time if I don't execute my plan to the "T". That's right, I have a plan. A pretty good plan too. I have to borrow some tips from Sage. He's the mastermind of situations like this. He always manages to get things to work out the way he wants them to. Drastic times call for drastic measures and this is drastic for sure. Ilesha and Rachel both disagree with the potential solution to my problem; however, I feel this move is the move I need to take. Hell, it's my life and I have to do what's best for me and my twins. They're counting on me to make things right. I will not fail.

Kevin is at In the Mix tonight with his boys celebrating the birth of his children. I'm sure they're having a good time. His friends are all pretty well off, so I know they are spending a lot of money and talking big. For some reason, guys get extremely excited when they have sons born. Maybe it's because they feel they have someone to carry on their legacy. Both Kevin and Eric take extra joy in knowing that they have a son. I know Kevin and his friends will be there all night long. I just hope they don't go overboard and someone drives irresponsibly.

Eric is out tonight too. He's going bowling with a few of his friends. That's his bread and butter. He's not really the type of person to do too much club hopping. He likes places that have more controlled environments. Not to say that that he doesn't go to bars and clubs, but it isn't a regularly occurring event. I don't mind one bit because I really don't want a man who's in clubs all the time anyway.

I am staying in tonight. I have to take care of my children. Now that I'm a mother, I will have to limit my nights out. The girls and I will still go out, but only on occasion. I have a responsibility to my children now. Clubbing every weekend will not allow me to be the best mother possible. Not to mention, my body has to get back in shape before I head back out. Motherhood is brand new for me and is nerve wrecking and exhilarating at the same time. Everyone's been very supportive and helpful throughout my pregnancy and short stint as a mother. My family and friends have shown an overwhelming amount of support. I wish my grandmother was around to see these two beautiful boys her granddaughter has given birth to.

Kevin sends me a text informing me that he's having a fantastic time at In the Mix. He says that people are buying rounds of drinks for him and the DJ there is shouting him out on his new fatherhood. He's feeling real good.

Eric wants to stop by after he finishes bowling to see me and the boys. I inform him that tonight is not good because I've already put the boys to sleep and will be asleep shortly too. I'm just so drained from taking care of my boys. There's always something to do. It seems like as soon as I change one diaper, it's time to change another. I'm constantly cleaning because I refuse to fall behind and let my house become a pigpen. I just can't have all that. When I'm not doing any of those things, I'm working on my body. Eric understands that I'm tired and makes plans to stop by tomorrow to visit with the boys. I feel guilty because I have both Eric and Kevin building bonds with a child who isn't theirs. I'll let them know when I feel the time is right, but for now it's time for sleep.

What the hell?! It's three o'clock in the morning and my doorbell is ringing off the hook and there's pounding on my front door. I don't know what's going on. I don't know if I'm still dreaming or if this is actually happening. I clear my head and realize that I'm awake and the noises I hear are real. I grab my phone to call 911 as I look out the window to see if I can tell who's banging on my door. When I look out the window, I see Eric's car in my driveway. I wonder why he would be here at this hour acting like this. Eric is going to get an ear full from me about this erratic behavior. He knows the boys are asleep. He needs to be more respectful of my house and my space.

I hurry downstairs to open the door to curse Eric out and I get the surprise of a lifetime. When I open the door, Eric and Kevin are both standing on my porch together. They both look extremely upset and ready to fight. Unfortunately, they don't look like they wish to harm each other; instead, it appears that I'm the focus of their aggression. If they're together, I have to assume they know what's going on. It's no big deal; the plan remains the same. It simply gets moved up a bit.

"Hi, guys. What are you two doing here at this hour banging on the door like mad men?" I ask.

"There's some bull shit going on and we're gonna get to the bottom of this shit right now!" screams Kevin.

Eric says, "You have a whole lot of explaining to do. You know why we are here. Don't play dumb with us!"

"Come in, but keep your voices down. The boys don't need to be awakened," I say.

"Fuck all that sleep shit. What's going on here?" asks Kevin.

"You two both seem to be upset, so let's get it all out on the table," I state.

Kevin reports, "You damn right I'm upset! I'm at In the Mix celebrating the birth of my sons and everything goes awry when this guy comes in," Kevin recounts the events of the evening as he motions toward Eric.

Kevin explains that he was at the club having a great time. At that time, Eric finished bowling and decided to go out with his friends for a couple of drinks. As luck would have it, he and his friends went to the same spot where Kevin was partying. The DJ announced congratulations to Kevin on having twins. One of Eric's friends told the DJ to announce that Eric also had a set of twins who were recently born.

A little later Sage, who runs In the Mix, gave Eric and Kevin a bottle of champagne to split as a celebratory gesture. While they were drinking the champagne, they began talking about their blessings. They also thought they recognized each other from the party at the Diamond Center. During the conversation, it became apparent that they both have a set of twins by the same woman. That woman is me. That damn Sage! Even when we're not together, he finds a way to fuck me!

They became irate when they put the information together and headed straight to my house. I guess I should have let Eric come over when he asked. He never would have gone to the club if he was here. Oh well, it's here in front of me now and I have to deal with it. It's time to pay up for my actions and see if I can make this incredible situation work out for me and my children.

"You are my fiancée and I demand some

answers. Tell us about the twins," says Eric.

"Fiancée! You're engaged to him? This just keeps getting fucking better and better. Who's the father of the boys?" Kevin asks.

"You may find this difficult to believe, but neither of you are the father of the twins. Eric, you are the father of Deric and Kevin, you are the father of Devin," I answer.

"Sheena, you are out of your damn mind! Stop playing around and give us some real answers," Eric demands.

Kevin replies, "This is not the time to be playing!"

I say, "I'm not playing. I am very serious. Let me explain."

"The floor is yours," Eric and Kevin say in unison.

I explain to them what was going on when I first met both of them. I tell them how I was dating them at the same time and fell in love with both of them without ever trying to be deceitful. The next thing I tell them is that in order to choose which one of them to pursue a relationship with, I planned to have sex with one of them and if it was good I would make my choice from there. I further inform them that my plan didn't work because I had sex with both of them within days of one another.

"At that time, I obviously released two eggs and as fate would have it, the sperm from both of you fertilized one egg a piece. That's how you both ended up being the father of one of them," I continue to enlighten them.

They're sitting here in complete silence and I'm unsure if that's a good or bad thing. They're both staring at me with blank looks. It's an uncomfortable silence in the room that's making it unclear whether they understand what I'm saying to them. To my dismay, Kevin stands up and flips my coffee table.

He screams, "This is unfucking believable! This is so unbelievable, that I don't believe it!"

I want to scream at the top of my lungs because he shouldn't be breaking things in my house, but the reason why he did it is understandable. This is a very emotional situation and I need to handle this tactfully.

I say, "I didn't believe it at first either, but it's legitimate. The truth is, I love both of you and that's the reason why I didn't cut ties with either of you. You are both great men and the fathers of my children."

"Yep, great men who you preyed on. What the fuck are we supposed to do with this information? Where the fuck do we go from here? The trust is gone and this relationship is broken. Sheena, tell me, what are we supposed to do now?" asks Eric.

"It can work. If the two of you will take a minute to calm down, I will tell you," I say.

Kevin states, "I don't want to hear another utterance from you. You are a lying bitch, just like the rest of these thots. I feel like a damn fool. You really had me sold. I thought you genuinely cared about me, but the truth is that you only care about yourself."

Eric immediately chimes in and says, "Kevin's right. You have to be pretty damn heartless to have us both thinking that you are interested in us when really you aren't. You are a self-serving, untruthful whore. There really is no other way to say it."

"I know I'm wrong for what I've done, but it's not like I'm the devil. I only did what men have been doing to women for years, hell centuries. You both are using some very harsh words to describe me that really aren't a true reflection of who I am. Furthermore, I won't allow you to call me out of my name," I explain.

Eric says angrily, "I got down on one knee to propose marriage to you and this is what I get for it. I feel violated ten times over. To top it off, all you can talk about is us calling you out of your name. A spade's a spade; it just is what it is. If the damn shoe fits, put the mother fucker on and wear it proudly."

I reply, "Wow! That was a deep dagger. I'm sure it doesn't cut nearly as deep as the wound I've given you, but I already apologized. We need to be rational adults and talk this out. If we calm down, we can resolve this dilemma."

"Fucking amazing! Now you want to discuss ways to resolve this situation. Your sneaky ass has had months upon months to have this discussion, but no, you played it from the angle that benefitted you the most. There was no regard for either of us or the twins. You are only sorry because you got caught. Now *that's* just like a man," replies Kevin.

"I guess neither of you have ever found yourself in an impossible predicament. Of course you haven't. I never intended for this to happen. I wanted to square things up, I truly did, but I ended up having sex with both of you and found myself in a quagmire of unimaginable proportions," I say.

"Yeah, yeah, whatever. You don't just accidentally end up fucking two men. That's an intentional act. You were dishonest and there is no other way to say it. You should just own it. At least that would be more respectable," Eric states.

I know I'm wrong. Shit, I'm dead wrong, but I'm not trying to beg and gravel. I apologized to them and they need to accept my apology. Damn, it's not like I shot one of them or something. They are men acting like two pieces of tissue. Men cheat on women all the time and expect us to bounce back immediately like nothing ever happened. I'm almost ready to kick both of them out of my house and just be done with this shit. Fuck it!

That's just the rebel side of me speaking. I know I need to make this right for my sons.

They will need their fathers in their lives. The world is a very tough place and they will need the guidance from people who have their best interests in mind. I messed this thing up, but it is what it is. I have to deal with it. My quest for love has backfired. I sought love and found it with two men. It's not meant for a person to be in love with two people, or is it? I have so many thoughts parading through my head that it's driving me crazy. I've never seen anyone as angry as Kevin and Eric are right now.

"Sheena! Are you listening to me?" Kevin asks.

I apparently drifted off in my own thoughts. I have no idea what he said. His eyes are bulging out of his head. I expect one of his eyes to pop out onto the floor. The veins in his forehead look like welts on a child after being beaten with a switch. I don't know what to tell him. He may become more infuriated if I tell him I wasn't listening, but I wasn't.

I respond, "I don't know what you said. I zoned out."

"You are a handful. Your attitude about this bull shit is so nonchalant. You have the audacity to tune me out and you are the one who is dead wrong. Unbelievable. You are unbelievable," says Kevin, as he shakes his head.

"My mind is racing a thousand miles per second. This is very serious to me. Don't be confused. I am devastated. Please, ask me again," I request.

"Devastated is an understatement. I am beyond words to explain how I feel. This is a very dark place that I've never been before. Unfamiliar territory. My emotions are raging like a bull right now," Kevin replies.

"I've never been here before either. I hoped to never be in an emotional state such as this," says Eric.

"My question is: Did you really expect for your plan to work? Did you? I mean seriously, how could someone so intelligent go forward with such a buffoonish act?" Kevin asks.

We have been arguing about the same thing for almost thirty minutes now. Tempers are flaring and we are saying things that we don't necessarily need to say. The only thing that could happen is for this to turn violent. Oh how I wish my girls were here right now. I would feel more comfortable if they were here with me because they would have my back. I'm clearly outnumbered right now.

I respond to Kevin's question by telling him it was a big mistake I made. That answer doesn't make him feel any better and seems to make the situation worse. I know he's angry and emotional, but this is out of hand. He keeps asking me the same damn questions over and over. He responds to my answers as he paces back and forth.

"I could strangle you right now. I mean wrap

my hands around your throat and squeeze until you breathe no more," says Kevin, while he demonstrates with his hands.

Eric states, "Physical harm. I am damn close to it too. If it wasn't for the twins, your ass would be cut like grass. I don't normally talk like this, but this entire fiasco is abnormal."

"Speaking of the twins, I'm getting a paternity test as soon as possible. I need to know for sure if I'm the father and prepare myself for what I may have to do," states Kevin.

"I totally agree with that," says Eric.

I explain to both Kevin and Eric that they don't need to get paternity tests. I go upstairs to my closet where I hid the results and bring them back downstairs. I let them peruse the results of their respective tests. They scrutinize every inch of the paper. Kevin is rubbing his chin and shaking his head, while Eric is rubbing his knee and clenching his fist tightly. They even switch results to review the other's.

"Do the results satisfy your need to have a paternity test?" I ask.

"Hell no. The probability of you having twins is slim and then when you add it the chances of you being pregnant by the both of us is damn near impossible," says Eric.

"Shit, for all we know, you could have been fucking someone other than us. He could be the father. For all I know, these results could be some shit you pulled off the internet to throw us off even more," says Kevin.

"Oh, you two are just too much. You are trying to play me out and I don't appreciate it. I am telling you that those results are certified. I did not forge them," I say.

"At this point, we don't believe anything you have to say. You probably got pregnant from some third party guy and he disappeared on you," replies Eric.

Kevin says, "Yeah, he probably doesn't work and has five other kids. A real deadbeat dad. Probably one of Ilesha's friends."

I immediately blast Kevin for even mentioning Ilesha's name. I have had enough of the insults. I will not allow disrespect to fall on me or any of my friends. My friends don't have anything to do with what I did. My decisions are exactly that - mine. That was a real bitch move because only a punk would bring up a person in an argument who isn't here to defend him or herself. I can't. I can't.

Kevin continues his rant, "Damn Sheena, you could've been honest about what you were doing. If a fuck is what you wanted, I still would have given you that. I just wouldn't have given you anything else. And then you come up with this outlandish story…"

I catch him mid-sentence and slap the shit out of him.

"I've had enough of the insults. I'm trying to understand how you feel, but disrespect is not tolerable by me. You have insulted me and my friends. You know I don't put up with that bull shit. Get the fuck outta my house, right now!" I exclaim. "I was trying not to get this way, but fuck both of you."

"Typical of a woman. She does wrong and now it's the man's fault for reacting. I'm out. I was just about to bounce anyway. Just when you think you've found the one, you get blindsided," says Eric.

"Stop babbling and get your sensitive ass out. I'm tired of listening to you two and your bull shit," I scream.

"No sweat off my back. Sisters are always talking about how full of shit men are, but the irony of the situation is that women are just as full of shit as men," says Kevin.

"I heard that," Eric cosigns Kevin's comment.

They both walk out of the door together. This is the day I dreaded the most. I knew at some point this would happen. In a funny way, I'm glad it happened. I can finally relax. I don't have to worry about my secret getting out. I'm now able to breathe easily and I don't have to secretly sleep with two men anymore. I was getting served some delicious dick though. I'll miss that part for sure, but this is for the best. All of the juggling was taking valuable time away from my boys.

I know I'm thinking ahead, but what will I tell my children when they are old enough to understand? They are twins, but have two different fathers. Will they judge me? Will they stop loving me because of what I've done? Will they want to leave me to go live with their fathers? Maybe I'm making this bigger than what it is. They are my children and they will love me unconditionally. Either way, I need to focus on the matter at hand, which is these two assholes.

"Did you just say: You heard that? What are you a fucking cheerleader?" I ask.

Eric shakes his head and gives me the middle finger as they approach their cars. How childish is that? He can't think that I really care about somebody flipping me the bird. I am from Linden, New Jersey and I've lived through far worse.

"Bye bitches! Go fuck each other!" I shout.

I honestly don't like being this way because it's so unlady like, but they pushed me. I don't let anyone talk to me disrespectfully. I will defend myself until the death of me if I have to. They needed to be dismissed anyway. I really don't like the way they popped up at my house with belligerent attitudes as if they were going to do something. They don't pay any bills and certainly don't run a damn thing at this residence. Hell, they didn't run anything in our relationships. I should have let them stand outside when they arrived and talk to each other, since they have each other's backs. They must be out of their damn minds coming over here like that. They will have hell to pay for disrespecting me and my house like that.

As soon as I close the door, I grab my phone to call Ilesha and Rachel and tell them to come to my house now. We need a face to face conference for this one. They should be here any minute. They know this is an emergency like no other, so they won't be long. I go upstairs to make sure my boys are sleeping comfortably. Devin is awake and is soaking wet.

"Mommy will take care of you," I say. "I'll have you cleaned up and changed in no time. You didn't even cry; you are an angel."

I finish changing Devin's diaper and hear the doorbell ring. My girls are here to support me as always. I head downstairs and open the door. Ilesha and Rachel walk in and we immediately share a group hug.

"So, the shit hit the fan, huh?" asks Ilesha.

"Yeah, the word definitely got to them," I respond. "And they came banging on my door like they had lost their damn minds."

"Oh my, girl! I know that was scary. I'm sorry we weren't over here to aid you in your time of need," says Rachel.

"Rachel please, you don't need to apologize. I was fine. They were nothing to deal with. Kevin and Eric reacted exactly how I thought they would. Hurling insults and very emotional. I'm surprised they weren't crying, especially Eric," I say.

Ilesha bursts out laughing from my comment and Rachel and I follow suit. I tell them what happened from the time Kevin and Eric arrived until the time I threw their asses out. They applaud me for the way I handled the situation. Rachel talks about how she would have been speechless as soon as she saw both of them outside of her house. I knew at some point they would find out or I would have to tell them. I wouldn't have been able to avoid the conversation forever.

We discuss many scenarios of how this will play out. The possibilities are endless. Also, we have differing opinions of how I should approach this one. Rachel, of course, wants me to reconcile matters.

"So, when are you going to call them to make amends?" asks Rachel.

Ilesha states, "She's not calling them at all. She has nothing to say to them."

"She has to consider the boys. She can't just proceed as if their fathers don't exist. It's not fair to keep their fathers from building a relationship with their sons," narrates Rachel.

"Ladies, thanks for deciding my life for me. You two will go back and forth over this all night if I let you. You know my boys will have their dads in their lives," I say.

"So what the hell you gonna do? Are you going to call them up and beg for forgiveness?" asks Ilesha.

"That's what I would do," says Rachel.

Ilesha responds, "You would because you're soft."

"You are pretty soft girl. You know it too. You apologize before you know you did anything wrong," I say lightheartedly.

Rachel defends herself by stating, "You both are mistaken. I am not weak; I'm smart. I just know the quickest way to resolve a dispute is to apologize and move on. I choose to exercise the option of apologizing instead of prolonging conflict."

"Ya ass can call it what you want, but I call that weak girl. I prefer not to settle the conflict. If a man wants to have conflict, then so be it. Let's be for real, no man can resist this juicy ass when I back it up on him," says Ilesha. "They always come crawling back. It's too damn good!"

We laugh and I enjoy this time with them. It's priceless. If your friends aren't there when you need them the most, they are not your friends. I appreciate their advice, but I have to follow my heart on this one. I have to live with this decision, so I will make it solely mine. I don't want my girls to harbor any guilt from following their advice and it doesn't work.

"I have a plan. You have to be willing to fight for love. I am willing to fight and make sacrifices. I don't want you to influence my decision, so I'm just going to do my thing. I hope you aren't offended by me not following your suggestions. I have to own this decision. It's all mine," I say.

My girls assure me that they fully understand why I have to do this my way. They inform me that I have their full support and to call on them whenever I need them. The boys begin crying; Rachel and Ilesha dart upstairs to see what's bothering their godchildren. I'll go upstairs soon, but I want Rachel and Ilesha to have some alone time with the boys. They visit with the boys for a while and then leave. As they're departing, Rachel jokes about her sleep being disrupted. A short while later I receive texts from Rachel and Ilesha notifying me they've arrived home and I can finally go back to bed.

CHAPTER 16

I'm awakened by the sound of raindrops beating against my window pane. It sounds like a small army marching closer and closer. I let out a long powerful yawn with both arms spread high above my head and fists tightly clenched. I am trying to get as much out of this yawn as I possibly can. I am very refreshed because my little angels allowed me to sleep through the rest of the night. They must have known their mommy really needed her rest last night. Even my babies have my back. Even though they are not crying out, I know they are looking for me.

I get out of bed and walk over to their crib. Just as I thought, the boys are awake and waiting patiently for their number one fan to come feed them. I change their diapers and clean them up. *Nice and fresh boys*, I think to myself as I kiss each of them on their cheeks. Time for breakfast.

"You want mommy to bring you your breakfast?" I ask.

Of course they don't respond, but I pull them out of their cribs and put them on my breasts. I'm very perturbed about what happened last night, but I will not allow an ounce of my anger to affect the way I treat my children. With that being said, their fathers will pay the price. Two wrongs don't make a right, but I damn sure will make it even.

I have a million things to do today. There is no way I can accomplish all of my tasks with the boys with me. All of the back and forth and getting in and out of the car with the boys will slow me down. Not to mention, it's pouring rain and they don't need to be out in this weather. Let me see which godmother is free to keep the boys for a while. I dial Rachel first and she answers.

"Hey girl," I say.

"Hey, I was just about to call to check on you," says Rachel.

"Girl, I'm good. I am not sweating that mess from last night," I respond.

Rachel replies, "You are so strong. I would still be a mess. You are my heroine. I wanna be like you when I grow up."

As I laugh, I ask, "What are you doing today?"

"I don't have anything planned. Why, do you need some girl time?" asks Rachel.

"Well, I actually I need some time to myself. I want to clear my head and I have a ton of running to do. I need you to keep the boys for me," I explain.

"I totally understand. I can keep the boys for you. I'll be home all day, so just bring them by when you're ready," Rachel replies.

"Thanks girl. I really need this time and it's too nasty to have the boys in and out of the car in this weather," I say.

Rachel replies, "Don't mention it. Just call when you get here and I'll open the garage."

I finish feeding the boys and get them dressed for their day with Rachel. I take a shower and get myself together to go out in this rainy weather. I load the boys and the things they need for the day into the car and drive over to Rachel's house. I drop the boys off and begin making my moves for the day.

I head to the office supply store to pick up some items needed for work. After that, I go to my office to drop the supplies off. My phone chimes to alert me that I have a message. It's a text from Eric. He wants me to call him as soon as I get a chance. I'm busy, so I guess I can't call him. There really is no chance in hell that I'm calling him.

The next destination on my list is to go to Kevin's house. He doesn't know I'm coming over, but it really doesn't matter to me. Since he thinks it's okay to pop up at my damn house, I'll return the favor. I pull into Kevin's driveway and leave the car running. I jump out of the car and run to the door to avoid getting drenched. Kevin clearly was in the window because he opens the door as soon as I approach it.

"I knew you would be by sooner or later," states Kevin. "I'm glad you stopped by."

I reply, "You may be glad I stopped by, but I don't understand why you are."

Kevin says, "I'm glad because you being here means you have chosen me. Eric and I figured whoever you came to visit first is the one you want to be with."

"That is hilarious. You two are fucking idiots. I don't want either one of your disrespectful asses," I say.

"If you are not here to make things right, then why are you here?" asks Kevin.

"Oh, I am here to make things right with you," I say.

When I say that, Kevin smiles as if he thinks I mean that he is the one I have chosen, but he couldn't be more wrong. I just told him that I didn't want either one of them and he still doesn't get it. It's amazing to me how men hear what they want to hear and think what they want to think.

"Well, come in and get out of the rain. We can talk inside where it's dry and warm," Kevin says.

"I won't be coming in. I'm good right where I stand. I don't want you. I do find it funny how you want to talk now, but last night when I wanted to talk, all you and your boyfriend wanted to do is yell and insult me," I report.

"Last night was very emotional and some things were said that maybe didn't need to be. Things kinda got out of hand," says Kevin.

I reply, "Kinda got out of hand is downplaying it. No things got way out of hand, but it's cool. I'm glad last night happened. It needed to and this needs to happen too."

I reach around my neck and take off the necklace Kevin gave me. I hold it in my hand and throw it to him. He catches the necklace and has a look of astonishment on his face.

"I don't want that shit anymore. Fuck you and your fig tree. I will do without it. You can melt that shit down into a bullet, put it in a gun, and kill yourself," I scream. "It wouldn't make me a damn difference."

"Sheena, you can't be serious. I don't want it back. I want you to have it," says Kevin.

"Too bad. That's bullshit to me now. I already told you what you can do with it and I meant that shit," I say.

Kevin runs from the door and down the steps. With the rain splashing off of his face, I can't tell if he's crying or not. To be honest, I really don't care. I jump back into my car and put it in reverse. Kevin is shouting for me to stop and to come back to chat. After I back the car into the street, I roll down the window and Kevin thinks he has gotten to me.

"Thank you, for stopping," he says.

"You said you want to talk?" I ask.

"Yes, I want to talk," Kevin replies.

"I have a conversation for you. Here it is… You should go fuck your new boyfriend Eric in the ass and then talk to him about whose ass feels better - his or mine," I retort.

I see Kevin's jaw drop so far that it was sitting on the top of his sneaker. I hit the gas and all you can hear is a loud screech. I literally left this asshole standing in a cloud of smoke. The smell of burnt rubber is not pleasant at all, but today I love it.

As I drive down the street, I look down at my phone. Eric has called me three times and left several voice messages. He has even texted me a few times. I decide to text him back to find out where he is. He's home, so I'm heading over to his house. I need to settle up with him too.

I arrive at Eric's and use my key to walk right into his house. Kevin and Eric ganged up on me last night, so now I'm ganging up on them. They will know after today that I am a one woman gang. I walk into his bedroom and drop a box on his floor. He's surprised to see me.

"I didn't expect you to come over. You didn't respond to the text I sent you after you asked me if I was home. Thanks for coming by," Eric says.

"No need to thank me. I came by for the boys, not for you," I say.

"I don't understand. What do you mean, for

the boys?" Eric asks.

I reply, "I mean the boys want me to drop off this stuff you bought for them. They don't want items from someone who isn't their father."

"Well, isn't one of the boys my son?" Eric immediately asks.

"You know at this point, I really don't know. It's like you and Kevin said last night, there's no telling who else I've slept with. I can't be sure who the father is, since I'm fucking all of D.C.," I say.

Eric says, "All we were saying is……"

"All you were saying is bullshit. You and Kevin had your dicks so far up each other's asses that you wouldn't listen to me. I'm cool with that because I don't need a damn thing from either one of you," I say.

"I plan to take care of my responsibility as a father. I will be an integral part of my son's life. You know that," Eric says.

"Umm, you don't tell me what I do or don't know. Also, you won't be a part of my son's life. You two were very clear that there is uncertainty about paternity. I will clear it up for you while I'm here," I state.

Eric is spinning in circles and is speechless. He begins to stutter while trying to talk because he is so mad. I'm amused about how he has no composure. He is unable to put his words together. I walk close to him and put my pointer finger on his lips to get him to stop mumbling. I instruct him to look me in the eyes and listen to me.

Once I have his attention, I look him in his eyes and say, "As Maury would say, YOU ARE NOT THE FATHER!"

Eric finally gets his words together and tries to convince me not to leave under these terms. He wants to come to a compromise of some sort. The time for compromise is over. It's about what I want and that's it. I tell Eric that me and the boys need a change of scenery. I tell him that there is no need to call, text, or stop by because we will be unavailable. I also let him know that he shouldn't buy gifts for my boys because their *father* may become upset.

"But you said last night that I am a father!" Eric screams.

"Again, you guys were right. The real father is a bum. You and Kevin were easy targets because you are both successful. So you don't have to worry about anything," I respond. "Yep, that's right. Don't worry about a thing."

"I am confused. You said I'm the father, now I'm not the father. Your story is changing constantly. This is exactly why I don't know what to believe," Eric says.

"I really don't care what you believe. Just know that me and the boys are out of here. You didn't even give me the benefit of the doubt when you came by last night. You just stuck to your negative thoughts about me," I say. "Eric, I also have one more thing to give you."

"What's that?" asks Eric.

I toss Eric his engagement ring. I throw it to him as if it is a piece of candy that really doesn't matter to me. He doesn't immediately recognize the ring in the air. When he looks in the palm of his hand after he catches it, his eyes tear up at the exact moment he realizes what it is. The ring is about as valuable as a plastic ring that comes out of a cereal box. The ring is beautiful, but doesn't mean anything to me at this moment.

I leave Eric's house in a storm, just the way I came in. He wants to talk further because he questions my new statements. Fuck him though. That sounds like a personal problem to me. I leave him hanging just as I did Kevin. I refuse to stay here wasting my time fooling with this cry baby. I still have other things I need to do before the day is over.

CHAPTER 17

My boys have gained plenty of weight since my last face to face encounter with their fathers. It seems like every pound they have gained, I have lost. It sounds so strange saying my twins have *fathers*. Kevin and Eric haven't stopped calling since the day I told them off and put them in their places. Kevin claims he can't live without me and Eric says that I am the love of his life. I know they miss my dazzling personality and sexual healing. I'm sure I have the grandest canyon they've ever put their dicks and faces in. I'll eventually let them be in my sons' lives, but they need to know that I am unwavering in my position on respect. For now, I will continue to hit them where it hurts. They can't live without me and they are absolute family men. The thought of losing me and their sons is horrifying to them. All of those nights of pillow talk have paid off tremendously.

I put a for sale sign in the front yard of my house. Kevin and Eric both have been calling and texting me incessantly about the nature of the sign. They are extremely concerned about where I plan to move and where their sons will be. The many inquiries are flooding my text message inbox. The voicemails have piled up so much that my voicemail message box is full. I don't delete them because I don't want them to be able to leave any more messages.

I text them back occasionally to let them know the boys and I are in Jersey. Kevin and Eric have both been dropping by my house and job to see if they can catch up to me. The boys and I are staying between Ilesha's and Rachel's houses. Kevin and Eric don't need to know that we were only in Jersey for a week to visit my family.

Kevin has left flowers at my doorstep, while Eric has left letters in the mailbox. I send Rachel or Ilesha to the house to check the mail. I don't want Kevin or Eric to catch me over there. They are definitely watching my house because they have commented via text about seeing my girls at the house.

They are borderline stalkers, but I'm kind of flattered that they are looking for me so intensely. Maybe I'm giving them too much credit. Kevin and Eric could just be angry that they can't reach me or the boys when they want. When Rachel saw the flowers Kevin bought me, she wanted to bring them to me immediately. Instead, I told her to leave the flowers on my doorstep, so they could die. I knew Kevin would be by the house again and see them dead on the porch. That act drove him wild and he called me at least fifteen times about those flowers, but I neglected to answer.

Eric's treatment has been the same over the last few weeks. The letters he has sent via mail have been returned to him unopened and the teddy bears are left outside in the elements. I'm sure the letters were very sweet and sentimental, but who cares. He'll just have to get over it.

I have intentionally created a competition by allowing Eric to see Kevin's gifts and Kevin to see Eric's gifts at my house. One day Kevin leaves a token of his love and the next day Eric leaves an even bigger and better present. They are both vying for my love and affection. I know their pride will not allow them to be outdone by the other, so I exploit their weakness. I really have to convince them that the boys and I are out of town and that I want nothing to do with them.

They both have been questioning me about when we'll be back, so they can schedule paternity tests. I simply respond to them by stating that they don't need to worry about when we'll be back. I inform them that if my house sells we won't be back and surely my kids aren't undergoing any type of DNA testing. They don't take that news lightly at all. I receive threats from them saying they are taking me to court for custody and all sorts of foolishness.

They must think I'm stupid. I know damn well that courts favor the mother. Even if they did take me to court, they would never get custody. The last thing either one of them wants is for the boys to be juggled around and divided. I just laugh out loud at the ridiculous comments they make.

I'm a hot commodity right now. I guess this is how the rules of supply and demand operate. When supply is low and demand is high, the price of the item goes up. Right now, Kevin and Eric want to see me, so my demand is high. Well of course I'm avoiding them, so that makes the supply low. Therefore, seeing me is of extremely high value. Talk about being in control. This is my airplane and I'm the pilot. It's time for takeoff.

Eric has administrative meetings at his school every Monday morning. During this meeting, he sets out a plan for the week with the assistant principals. They discuss everything pertaining to the school. The main purpose of the meeting is to ensure everything flows smoothly for the week. He never misses the meeting. I call him when I know he is well into his meeting. I don't want to talk to him, but I want him to know I called. If for some odd reason he answers, I will just tell him that I butt dialed him. It wouldn't be the first time I accidentally dialed someone. Just as I suspect, he does not answer the call. I'm not leaving a message.

Kevin is normally unavailable during the early part of his workdays. He's often in meetings or on conference calls. I extend him the same call that I gave Eric. Again, I know he isn't going to answer either. The phone rings several times before going to voicemail. I hang up once the recording engages.

Since the night they showed up at my house, I have not been the first one to call or text. I'm sure they will be utterly surprised when they notice I've reached out to them. They will also wonder what made me finally call. I will not answer the phone when they call back. I know they will want to slap themselves for missing my call.

An hour later I get a call from Eric, but I don't answer. He immediately calls back. I only allow the phone to ring once before I hit the decline button that directs him to my full voicemail. I know this is ticking him off because he knows for sure that I intentionally didn't answer his call. I won't talk to him until the latter part of the week. Kevin also reaches out to me. His phone calls also go unanswered by me. They are both stewing in the fact that they missed my call.

I respond to their texts and tell them I'm busy and will get back to them when I'm free. I lead them to believe that I'm in New Jersey looking at properties to live in and a new location for my business.

I allow a few more days to pass with Kevin and Eric constantly calling me. I have to play this just right. They are feeling a sense of urgency to see me right now, so they will come running as soon as I make myself available. I know their minds are spinning like a twister because there are so many questions they need answers to. They will have the answers I provide for them soon enough. In fact, Saturday night works for me.

The big day is here and I spend the early portion of the day getting my nails and hair done. I also hit the mall and pick up on a few new pieces. Ilesha has the boys for the duration of the day and night. I decide to call Kevin first and he answers before the first full ring is complete.

"Hi, I have been waiting for your call. We need to talk," says Kevin. "This situation is really out of hand."

"Well I'm done talking, but I'll be home at eight tonight for about an hour. Come by then," I say.

As I expected, he tries to hold a conversation over the phone. I shut that down real quick and hang the phone up. He will show up tonight for sure because he wants to unload. I call Eric next.

"Hey," I say when he answers the phone.

"Wow, I'm surprised to be hearing from you. You are a very hard lady to catch up to these days," Eric states.

I say, "I'll be home tonight at eight. Stop by then. Don't be late. I'll only be there for about an hour to pick up some things and then me and the boys are headed back to Linden for a while. I don't know when we'll be back again."

I hurry him off the phone. Of course, we're not heading back to Linden tonight or anytime in the foreseeable future. I know men and how they move. They won't miss a chance to see me and the boys. I'm sure they'll be surprised to see each other when they arrive.

It's eight o'clock sharp when I look out the window and notice that both Kevin and Eric are on my porch. Eric rings the doorbell, but I don't open the door promptly. After a few minutes of them waiting on the porch, I am ready for them to come in. I finally open the door and allow the two of them the pleasure of setting their eyes on such a magnificent feast.

I have vanilla scented candles burning and a playlist full of slow songs playing softly in the background. The mood I have set in my living room is totally contradictory to what they expected it to be. This is a living room of pure seduction. I know they're confused and wondering if this is for them or someone else.

I have two glasses of wine set up on the coffee table along with a bottle of wine. I'm wearing an all-black gown with a deep V-line cut that perfectly highlights my plump breasts. The dress has a sexy split that goes up to my hip and I've paired it with some sexy Red Bottom stilettos. I'm completely oiled up with smells of strawberry. Kevin and Eric's eyes follow the curves of my gown as I stroll back and forth. This dress is hugging all of the right places and flowing seductively in others.

"Guys, it's great seeing you. It seems like it has been forever since we've last seen each other," I say.

Kevin says, "It's great seeing you too, but I didn't expect this. The candles, the music....."

Eric interjects Kevin while he is talking and states, "I agree. We have some major issues that need to be resolved and it appears you're playing romance night. Are you expecting someone else?"

I respond, "No, I'm not expecting anyone else. Please sit down and have a glass of wine."

I didn't have to offer the wine twice to Kevin. He immediately chugs down one glass and is pouring another. I'm certain he's smitten by how great I look and only hopes he's able to taste me again.

"Since the last time the two of you were here was such a hostile encounter, I figured I would set a different tone. Sit down on the couch and listen to me for a minute. I've been doing a lot of thinking about our situation and I believe we can make this work," I state as we sip wine.

"How, Sheena? How can this work?" Eric questions.

"We can make this work by being a family. The boys need to grow up together like brothers should. They also need their fathers to be a part of their lives daily. Let's make it work for them. We can do this. If we can't make this work, I will just have to move the boys with me back to my hometown to be near my family," I narrate.

"So, you brought us here to tell us you're leaving," Eric inquires.

"No, I brought you here to discuss our options. I genuinely love you and want to be with you," I explain.

Kevin stands abruptly and asks, "So how do you feel about me? Are you saying you don't love me?"

"Kevin, have a seat," I say in a calm voice.

Kevin sits back down on the couch. I sit in between the two of them as we talk. I explain to Kevin that I still love him too. This situation is without a doubt crazy. I probably wouldn't believe it if I wasn't living it. But this is where we are and we need to deal with it. I rub Kevin's face gently and look him in the eyes and let him know we can get through this. I turn to Eric and wipe the tears off of his face.

I kiss Eric on his lips as I tell them it can work. As I'm kissing Eric, he is turning his face away. He's trying to avoid my advances, but I see him giving in because he really wants me. He eventually begins to kiss me back. It's amazing what the body will do when it wants something.

While Eric is kissing me, I'm groping Kevin's dick outside of his pants. He's dick is as hard as a barbell and his eyes are rolling back in his head. He's had a few drinks, so his defenses are at a minimum anyway. I take Eric's head and push it into my breasts. He sucks my tits as I stroke his meat with one hand and continue to stroke Kevin's meat.

"Pull it out of your pants," I demand.

They both reach down for their belt buckles and before long, both of them have their dicks out. I lick Eric's rod as he sits on the couch and I stroke Kevin's. I then switch to sucking Kevin's rod. I have them both where I want them. I look up at Kevin, while I'm licking his balls.

"I want you to hit it from the back, now baby," I say.

Kevin jumps up immediately and bends me over. While he's hitting it from the back, I take Eric's tool and place it between my boobs. I vacillate between sucking his dick and letting him titty fuck me. We are getting it in and I'm in ecstasy. I can't believe how fantastic this feels. Double the pleasure!

Kevin and Eric are both moaning and grabbing my body. Kevin is pumping me so hard from the back that I have to stop sucking Eric's dick because I might bite him. I know Eric needs to get some of this action, so I wait for Kevin to slip out of me and then I sit on Eric's dick. I wrap my hands around his neck and slowly grind on him. Then I speed up and tighten my grip around his neck and bounce my tight juicy ass off his dick.

"Kevin, smack me on my ass! Smack it, damn it! Smack it!" I order.

Kevin smacks my ass just how I like it. I turn around and ride Eric reverse cowgirl. I grab Kevin's meat and put it in my mouth, while I serve Eric.

"I love you baby," says Eric. "You make me feel like nobody else ever has."

I look back and say, "I love you too Bae."

Kevin's legs are starting to wobble, so I know he is getting ready to burst. I feel Eric getting a firmer grip on my hips as I ride and he's speeding up, so I know he's ready to explode too. I ride his dick faster, so his release can be intensified and as far as giving Kevin head, I suck him faster and deeper until he creams in my mouth. They both release at the same time and I'm all smiles.

I say, "This is how we can make it work. I will be in a relationship with both of you. There's no getting around the fact that I have a child by both of you. We can all be happy together. You both can have me, I can have you, and the boys will have their dads. I don't think any of us want the alternative. Let's give it a shot."

Eric says, "I do want you, but this is not what I had in mind."

"Yeah, I don't know about this Sheena. This is a bit over the top," says Kevin.

"Fellas, it's a new day and the days of the traditional family are seemingly over. If a homosexual or lesbian couple can raise a family, why can't we raise our kids together? This isn't abnormal. People live in polyamorous relationships all the time and they don't have kids together," I explain. "We have more at stake, so we will make it work."

"Everything she's saying is legitimate. The family structure is rapidly changing. I'm willing to try it. If this will keep my son near me, I am down with it," says Kevin.

Eric says, "I'll give it a shot because I can't live without you Sheena. I also want to be a part of my son's life every day. As crazy as this may sound, I would rather share you, than to not have you at all."

I say, "My boys get to have their fathers around daily and we get to have each other too. Everyone wins here. Guys, now that we are on the same page, let's go upstairs for some more adult action. I'm ready for round two."

EPILOGUE

I know polyamorous relationships may be a bit extreme to many, but life is all about getting what you want. Sometimes you have to go the extra mile to get what you want out of life. I met two great guys basically at the same time and was unwilling to let either one of them go. I am not ashamed of what I'm doing. I have the best of both worlds. Each man is what the other man is not. They make me whole and they are both serving me all I can handle. I'll explain to my boys when the time is right what exactly is going on and how things transpired or maybe I won't. As long as there is love in the house, there may be no need to explain anything.

I never had any intention to move the boys away from their fathers. I had to say something to get them to agree to what I wanted. I hit them where I knew it would hurt the most. The love of a child and a woman are two powerful emotions and are hard to overcome. I knew they wouldn't let us walk away without a fight.

Maybe some of you will consider me a slut and that's cool. I'm sure we all have done some questionable things in our lives, so if you are judging me, you are judging yourself too. Deep down I always had a fantasy of being with two men at one time and now my fantasy comes true when I want and on my terms.

I feel empowered. I played the men, instead of

them playing me. If a man had two women living with him, he would be an icon to his peers. Women, if you want it, go get it; we can be icons too. Live on your terms and be strong and resolute in what you do.

www.ingramcontent.com/pod-product-compliance
Lightning Source LLC
Chambersburg PA
CBHW071005280626
47160CB00015B/1379